Peacekeepers

A Humboldt Love Story

Humboldt State University Press

Humboldt State University Library

1 Harpst Street

Arcata, California 95521-8299

hsupress@humboldt.edu

digitalcommons.humboldt.edu/hsu_press

Cover image art by Jeff Conner

Cover design and layout by Kim Sisu

ISBN: 978-1-947112-67-4

Peacekeepers

A Humboldt Love Story

Jeff Conner

Humboldt State University Press

Chapter One

Small Mill Town

September 16, 1996, 1423 Hours

Officer Mark Coltrane was sweating. He could feel little trickles run down his back, underneath his ballistic vest. It was a warm day in September. He was standing outside the lumber mill in Small Mill Town. He was dressed in what little riot gear his small department owned and wearing a borrowed helmet. Theoretically, he was there to protect the mill from the thousands of protesters lining the shoulders of the highway. But he thought it was more likely he was there because his sergeant was pissed at him. Today was his "weekend" and here he was working an overtime shift. Yes, he would get paid for it, but Uncle Sam would take his share, he would likely lose five pounds in fluids, and his feet would ache by the end of the day. He wasn't happy; he was bored. He let his mind run. He daydreamed. He wrote letters in his head. Maybe when this was over, he would try and get some of the better thoughts on paper. All the while he watched the protesters.

They seemed to come in numerous flavors. There were the liberal elite, who lived out of the area, but had the means to travel to Big Tree County to protest the possible logging of the last remaining large stand of old-growth redwood. They wore outdoorsy clothes from major labels that looked like they had never felt a whitethorn bush. There were members of the Sierra Club who had driven or flown to this location, some from a great distance, despite the carbon footprint it caused. There were college kids by the score, some from the local university and more from elsewhere. But few, if any of them, had the responsibilities that came with adulthood. They were able to spend their time as they pleased, at least until the future caught up with them.

And then there were the "dirty hippies" as they tended to be called by his comrades in arms. They were the locals of EPIC (Environmental Protection Information Center) and Earth First. He had first met their ilk when he worked in the woods. He had encountered them locked to the gate that accessed his crew's work site, just a few miles from here. They had detoured and entered Big Timber Company's timberlands through a different gate, causing him to fire up his Cat about an hour later than the normal 6:00 AM start time. But the protest had caused no other disruption. These people were in many ways the most interesting. Interesting in a law enforcement capacity, because if anything requiring extra energy was called for, they were likely to be the cause. He respected determination and these folks had been fighting this battle for years. They had won some fights and lost others, but they seemed just as determined today as they had been five years ago when he first saw them.

Mark thought he had a better idea of what was happening here than most of the participants on either side of the police line. He had studied forestry and worked in these woods. He had seen abysmal forestry in the name of profits. He had run over thousands, nay tens of thousands, maybe even hundreds of thousands, of seedlings and saplings to get to the carcasses of the few remaining old-growth stems in what had been called seed tree or shelter wood cuts. When he had finished building layouts with his dozer, big pillows of soil to cushion the fall of the giant trees, the slopes were devoid of vegetation and covered with loose soil. He knew that some of that soil would be carried by surface flows into the nearby stream courses when it started to rain. And it rained here a lot. The sediment would destroy fish breeding habitats and cause flooding downstream. But that was all secondary to profit.

But Mark also knew that Big Tree County, especially the alluvial flats, was one of the best areas in the world for growing trees, for producing lumber. And that clear-cutting, when done properly, was the most efficient way to grow and harvest timber. He was embarrassed by the poor forestry he had participated in, but also thought that if logging was slowed or stopped in this area, it would only move the production to other parts of the world where logging practices were several times worse. This was private land, what right did these people, these thousands of people, have to stop what was still a legal process? He wanted to see compromise, to see better forestry, but to allow logging to continue. Preservation was another issue. He knew where the Headwaters Forest, the basis for this protest, was located. He knew that few people, other than some diehard locals, would ever visit the old growth stand; it should be the trees that are protected in perpetuity. Did that make any difference? There were already thousands of acres of protected old-growth forests along the main highways. How much was enough? He knew enough to know that there wasn't a simple answer to this question. And so Mark stood still, watching the crowd and feeling the sweat run down his back and into his soggy underwear.

There were some interesting moments. A cop he knew a couple of places down the line saw an old friend in the crowd and left his place to give his friend a hug. The sound of, "Get your fucking ass back in line" rang from a sergeant. The cop continued his hug for a moment and then coyly smiling, returned to his place in the line. The huggee giggled, smiled back, and teasingly played with her hair. There were pickup trucks that would drive past with men in the back brandishing chainsaws. They would slow, the chainsaws would rev and the truck would continue down the highway. They had placards like, "Earth First, we'll log the other planets later" attached to the sides. And there were protesters dressed as owls who would hurl insults at both the passing loggers and the line of police officers that blocked their access to the mill. But every time one of the owls got close to Mark, he noticed a woman would move from the crowd and place herself between the owl and the police. He started to watch her, wondering about her motivation. What had caused her to take this role? She was young, maybe in her early twenties, average height, athletic build. She had blonde hair worn in a ponytail and it bobbed and weaved as she patrolled her section of the protest. She wore a teal-colored T-shirt with the word "Peacekeeper" stenciled on it. And she was attractive, maybe not stunningly beautiful, but she looked good from a distance. And as he continued to watch her, he noticed that there were other persons, similarly dressed, that were performing much the same function at other places in the line. How nice to have a well-organized, time wasting, protest.

The day wore on, his underclothes were soaked. His head felt like it was being baked in an oven. Mark saw the pickup, but paid it little extra attention as it looked like all the others that had driven by. And then he noticed the man riding in the back. This was a violation of course, but the Highway Patrol seemed to be absent, at least when it came to the counter-protesters. He had seen a Toyota with several protestors in the back pulled over when he arrived, but the traffic cops were nowhere to be seen now. The man looked familiar and then Mark recognized him. His name was Dave and he had worked with him in the woods. He had thought the guy was an asshole then, so it didn't surprise him much that he was here. The truck slowed just as a couple of owls approached the cop next in line to him. Peacekeeper did her thing and started to move to intervene. His attention was focused on her, why wouldn't it be? She was an attractive young woman, and he wasn't dead yet. But out of the corner of his eye, he saw Dave throw something towards the crowd. His focus shifted. Before he could vocalize a warning, he identified the flying object as a water balloon. It was hot, who would really care? And in the time, it took to form that thought, it was too late to take any action other than watch. The balloon arched gracefully through the air and started the earthward portion of the parabola that was its flight path. He thought it would miss everyone, but Peacekeeper, who appeared to be completely focused on her job, was still moving to head off a confrontation. And that movement took her directly into the downward path of the balloon. It struck her on the side of her head just above the ear and as intended, it burst, showering her with fluid. But he had been wrong. The smell told him this. It was not a water balloon. Rather it was filled with a different fluid, an insulting and degrading fluid, and a more dangerous fluid. Dave had filled the balloon with urine, and it was not particularly fresh urine.

Peacekeeper stopped briefly, as did everyone else around her. But after gathering herself for a second or two, she continued her movement, placing herself between the owls and the police line. The owls had stopped yelling insults. They stood still, unmoving. When they failed to heed her request to move back with the other protesters, she gently pushed them away from the police. The smell may have been more effective than her physical efforts. And then she spoke softly into a radio she wore on her belt. He saw her release the press-to-talk button and heard a softly muttered, "Fuck, shit, piss."

Mark reached into the cargo pocket on the thigh of his duty pants and removed a bottle of water and a towel. He had used the towel to try and hold back some of the sweat rolling down his face. But he had given up a long time ago and stuffed the towel back in his pocket. While it was slightly damp, given the situation, he didn't think she would care very much. "Hey, Peacekeeper," he called. He knew this was a violation of policy. He wasn't supposed to talk to the protesters. But fuck it, this woman had urine in her hair; he was a cop, and at least as far as he was concerned, he was supposed to help people in need. She turned, a slight look of surprise on her face. He held out the towel and the water. They approached each other, meeting in front of the police line. He handed her the items, and she took them, still wearing the surprised look. She started to pour the water over her head.

"No wait, bend over first, otherwise it will just run down into your clothes. Here, let me help you." He spoke the words without thought. He took the bottle from her yielding grasp and had her bend over slightly. He poured the water slowly over the side of her head and when the first was empty, he opened a second. He used the towel to keep the water from flowing down her neck and into her T-Shirt. When he was done, the worst of the smell was gone and her shirt was still dry, more or less. She stood, faced him, her lips formed a thin smile, and she mouthed the words, "Thank you." Her eyes scanned his uniform and then she added, "Thank you very much, Officer Coltrane." He took the last item from his cargo pants: a plastic sandwich bag that contained the remains of a roll of toilet paper. "This is the cleanest thing I have to wipe your face with," he told her as he offered her the bag. She looked at the bag and then at him. The smile deepened and spread across her whole face. And he realized that he had been wrong again. For she was stunningly beautiful. It was her eyes that fulfilled this description. They were a bright, sparkling blue. Eyes you could get lost in. And he did.

Their brief reverie was broken by two men. One wore a blue uniform and had chevrons on his sleeves. The other wore a teal T-shirt similar to Peacekeeper's and carried a second shirt. Both men were hurrying to their location. The couple, for they had shared something, though neither knew just what, broke apart and faced the oncoming member of their "team."

"What the fuck are you doing, Coltrane?" screamed the sergeant, far more outraged than warranted.

Mark's response was an attempt at calm, a simple, "Well, sergeant, this woman was the victim of a crime. I was tending to her injuries and taking her statement. Was that inappropriate?"

His response was a bellowing, "That fucking bitch got what she deserved; now get your ass back in line."

"I beg to differ, sergeant. No one deserves to be pelted with urine. What's your fucking problem?" was his angry retort.

He realized that his position was ironic. He was on the edge of the protestors, facing the police line. He was swearing at a police officer, an officer who was pig-headed, pun intended, and couldn't understand that his world was changing. Mark wondered if he would need to be looking for a new job shortly. And out of the corner of his vision, he saw people converging on him once again. There were multiple people in teal shirts as well as officers of the law. But these officers didn't wear chevrons; they had jewelry on their collars. He didn't know who was going to help him more, the peacekeepers or the command staff.

His thoughts were broken when an owl gave him a hard shove in the back and yelled, "Get out of here you fucking pig." As he was propelled towards the police line, he saw the sergeant start to reach for his baton. Behind him, he heard a loud guffaw, but that was quickly replaced by,

"Shut the fuck up and get back behind the line." Apparently, a few of the peacekeepers were aware of the assistance he had rendered to one of their own. And in front of him, just as it was going to get ugly, a captain from the Sheriff's Department showed up. He knew her by reputation, tough as nails, and no one was going to mess with her. Maybe, just maybe, she was the perfect person to handle this.

"What's going on here, Sergeant?" she asked in a calm voice. He could not hear the sergeant's reply as it was muted by the roar of the crowd. Bonnie Raitt had appeared.

The captain then turned to him and asked, "Are you ok?" He nodded his head in response. She nodded in return and stated, "Then return to the line, things might get a bit more interesting now." She led the sergeant away as Mark took his place, once more facing the crowd. They all knew that if things were going to go sideways, it would happen now that the media cameras were here.

But it didn't. Instead, the protest moved down the paved, but private haul road that led to Logging Camp, Big Timber's corporation yard. Most of the cops drove on the County road to get there ahead of the crowd. He knew he was going to have to walk. Yet he didn't mind so much. For now, he had someone to look for. He would get occasional glimpses of Peacekeeper from a distance, but there was never the opportunity to share a word or a smile. The walk ended after about two miles. He was assigned a perimeter post and watched as those protestors who wanted to get arrested formed a line. A line of cops, formed at a right angle to the protestors and just inside the gate, was there to meet them. As each arrestee crossed the property line they were met by the next officer in line. They were taken into "custody," hand cuffed using disposal flex-cuffs, and walked over to a table to be booked by correctional deputies from the jail. Afterwards, the officer would return to the end of his line. The arrestees had their flex-cuffs snipped, signed a promise to appear, and were returned to the crowd. But everyone knew that it was entirely symbolic. The District Attorney's Office would never file charges on any of the protestors. It was all quite civilized and orderly. He was too tired to try and figure out if it was a waste of time or not. The process continued until after dark when he was finally released from duty and told to get a couple of hours sleep before he needed to be back at work in the morning.

Peacekeeper was gone. Apparently, it wasn't meant to be.

Chapter Two

Big City

October 25, 1996, 2152 Hours

Mark's bladder felt like it was going to burst. He had been driving for six hours straight and drinking down Diet Cokes the whole way. He still had at least fifteen minutes before he was home and he didn't know if he would make it or not. He saw the sign for the restaurant ahead. He had eaten there before, but not often. The food was ok, typical coffee shop fare. But the waitresses— and he couldn't ever remember seeing a waiter— all wore short, black skirts. He had forgotten to grab any road food and his stomach was telling him that it was time to eat. He had been gone for a week, so it was unlikely that there would be anything worthwhile in the fridge at home anyway. He moved into the left turn lane and pulled into the parking lot.

He went through the front door and smiled at the hostess. She looked like she was maybe sixteen and he felt like a dirty old man when she bent down to pick up a dropped menu and his gaze followed her. But if that's what he was, he was going to own it. He smiled, asked about the bathroom and received directions. The bathroom was clean, well clean enough, and the management was considerate enough to put the sports page of the local paper on the wall above the urinal. He wasn't real interested since baseball season was over, but he glanced at the articles on local high school sports. It took a while for his bladder to empty, and when he was done he washed his hands. Not just because it was good hygiene, but because he had spent most of the day shooting at the firearms instruction class he had just attended. The residue left by his weapons was pretty unhealthy and he wanted to make sure his hands were clean before eating.

He returned to the lobby and the hostess led him to a table. He sat, a bit surprised that the restaurant was so empty. He looked at his watch and realized that it was almost 10pm. No wonder he was hungry. He looked at the menu. He felt like red meat— a hamburger would be safe. It's pretty hard to screw up ground meat cooked all the way through. But he decided to take a risk and get a steak. He knew it would be frozen and not the best grade, but he wanted real meat. The waitress arrived as he put down his menu. Her name tag said Tammy. She was about eighteen, cute and wore the obligatory short, black skirt. He smiled, and because she kind of had to, she smiled back. He placed his order and admired Tammy's derriere and legs as she walked away. Then he reached for his book. It was a military thriller. He started to read. He had always enjoyed reading, but since the previous December, he spent significantly more time with his eyes focused between the pages. And now he read more fiction, which hadn't always been the case. He found that he needed to escape from his life and fantasize about another more than ever before.

His meal came and he thanked the waitress with two words and a smile. The feeling was genuine, and he returned to his book without even a glance at the departing young woman. The steak was surprisingly good and covered with an herb rub. Tammy returned several times to fill his glass of Diet Coke as he ate his meal and then cleared away his dishes. He smiled repeatedly, but stayed engrossed in his book. Tammy did not seek conversation either, leaving him in peace. He read on; the story having become rather engaging. He felt, rather than saw or heard, a person slide into the booth across the table from him. There was a faint odor in the air, he knew that he had smelled it before, but he could not place it. As he looked up, he heard the words, "We're closing in five minutes."

His eyes met hers. They were still the most amazing blue he had ever seen. The recognition was instantaneous. His smile broadened into a kind of grin. She wore a black leotard top with a large scoop neck. The straps of her black bra were visible on her shoulders. He could see ample portions of her breasts above the dark material. But his eyes stayed locked on hers. He assumed that she too, wore a short, black skirt. "Hello Peacekeeper. To what do I owe the pleasure of your company?" he asked.

"We're closing in five minutes. Tammy told me I could bring you your check. We need to clear your table so we can go home," she responded.

He looked around. Apparently, he had been more engrossed in his book than he realized. He was the only one still sitting at a table. The chairs had all been placed on top of the tables. Tammy was sweeping at one end of the dining room, while another young woman in a short, black skirt, twirled a mop from side to side.

"I'm sorry, I lost track of the time."

"Apparently," was her retort.

He looked at her closer. She was much younger than he was. He'd guess college age if he had to, but it was kind of hard to pin down. She had an elliptical face, framed by her blonde hair. She still wore it in a ponytail, but he wondered if that was because of her job. He liked the vision that came to him of her loose hair surrounding her face and cascading across her shoulders. She wore large, dangling earrings. He couldn't make out the shape, but they contained lots of colors on a silver metal. A simple pendant hung from her neck. But he couldn't pull his vision away from her eyes. A part of him seemed to be lost there. She didn't flinch from his gaze, meeting it with her own. She slid a check, face down, across the table to him and then stood up and left.

He watched her walk away, and he wanted to think that his gaze was one of admiration rather than lechery. Ok, maybe it was a bit of both. She did wear a short, black skirt. She had black tights on underneath. Her hips had a rather seductive wiggle and then she was gone around a corner. He grabbed the check and his book and headed for the cash register by the door. As he got to the register, he looked at the bill and reached for his wallet. He handed the check to the hostess, but as he did so, he noticed something written across the stub at the bottom. He asked the hostess for the receipt, claiming it was for his tax records. She tore it off and handed it to him, then took his money. He returned to his table and left Tammy a generous tip. He wondered if they shared tips here. He dropped another ten dollars on the table. It was only fair as he had kept them all from going home early.

As he walked to the door, he looked at the little piece of paper in his hand. In addition to the amount of his bill, there were seven numbers scrawled across the bottom. He smiled. The first three numbers were the same as the first three numbers of his home phone. He placed the receipt in his wallet.

She was a beautiful woman. He was— well, he didn't consider himself all that attractive. He liked who he was, knew he was a good man, but good looking? That wasn't him. His fitness had returned with all the running he had been doing, but he was still overweight, carrying 275 pounds on his frame. These thoughts whirled through his mind as he headed outside. And then, there she was. Her hair was loose, as he had envisioned. It did indeed flow around her face and cascade across her shoulders. Her face was lit softly by a streetlamp. She was even more beautiful in this light than he had thought. He didn't know what to say, so he didn't say anything. Instead, he just looked into her eyes where it was too dark to see the color, but he could tell that they were smiling. They stayed this way for what seemed like minutes, but was probably only fifteen seconds or so. He finally said, "Let me walk you to your car."

She turned and headed towards the back of the parking lot where he followed. She opened the door of a beat-up pickup, not what he expected. As she did so, she turned and faced him. It was darker here, but there was just enough light to see her face, although it was filled with shadows. He was good at reading body language; it was part of his job, and he saw the question cross her features. Then she leaned forward and gave him a quick kiss on the cheek. As she turned to enter her truck, she whispered, "Call me."

The truck started and was gone. He hadn't moved since her lips had grazed his skin. He was stunned. This had never happened to him before. He had never met a woman who was so aggressive about what she wanted. Had things changed that much in the last fifteen years? Were all young women this bold, or was it just this one? And what the hell did she see in him? As he headed towards his car, he toyed with the ring on his finger. Was it time to take it off? It had been more than ten months. Had she seen it? Did she care? So many questions.

He found his car and pointed it towards home. His mind was not on his driving. Instead, he found himself focusing on her face, on the quizzical look before she kissed him. His car managed to find its own way home and pulled into his driveway. His roommates were already asleep, but his best friend, Gunner, met him at the door. His short stub of a tail looked like a metronome gone crazy. Mark took a quick shower and then crawled into bed, his own bed. It felt right after a week on the road. It felt even better when Gunner laid down beside him, his head resting on leg. Mark's eyes closed and his last thought of the day was of a beautiful young woman.

Chapter Three

College Town

October 26, 1996, 0847 Hours

The next morning, he woke up and began his chores. He cleaned up the kitchen, started his laundry, and did a little yard work. But the whole time the receipt with the phone number was tugging at the edges of his mind until it took center stage. He pictured her while he worked. He admitted that he liked the picture. Her smile spoke volumes; it was coy, yet intriguing. But that was just a small part of the elation that was slowly building inside of him. Someone thought that he was interesting, interesting enough to take a risk, to put themselves out there, and to risk embarrassment. And this person was young and beautiful. He couldn't fathom what she saw in him. He was honored, but a bit confused.

He ate a late lunch and then he just couldn't stand it any longer. He took out the receipt and dialed the number he found there. He didn't know what he was going to say. He had elected, like he did a lot of times, to just wing it. After all, what could go wrong? The phone rang once, twice, three times and then four. He heard the connection go through and was about to say hello, but he realized that it was an answering machine. It wasn't her voice. He was sure that he had dialed the correct number, so when he heard the beep, he simply stated, "Hey Peacekeeper, it's the Cop. Tag, you're it." And then he left his phone number.

He could feel the adrenaline rush subside and he wondered if this was just a game or maybe some kind of sick joke. After all, she had been on the other side of the protest line. He could feel a cold, blue lump form in his chest. And after where he had been, that wasn't a welcome feeling. He went to the stereo and found the disk he was looking for. It was the soundtrack to the movie *Forrest Gump*. He had first seen this movie less than a month after Karen died, and he had never cried so hard as when Forrest had tried to run off the grief of Jenny leaving. He had actually sobbed out loud in the movie theater. Forrest may not have been very smart, but he definitely knew what love was. And Jenny, well, she was pretty clueless until it was too late. But that's another story. The soundtrack had become his go to music when he needed an emotional release. His roommates were gone so he turned it up until he could feel the vibrations and the windows began to rattle. He hoped his neighbors were tolerant. He played snippets of some songs, skipped others entirely. And then he got to Gladys Knight and the Pips. The bass drum began to pound and the horns began to play. This was what he was waiting for. He accompanied Ms. Knight as best he could. What he lacked in talent, he tried to make up for with volume. This was a song about a lover's betrayal, a form of grief all its own and different than his. But there were two verses that described how he had felt perfectly:

Peacekeepers

Darkness all around me
Blackin out the sun
Old friends call me
But I just don't feel like talkin to anyone

Emptiness has found me
And it just won't let me go
I go right on livin'
But why I just don't know

The words resonated now as they had for what seemed like forever. And as the Pips faded, he realized that he was crying. He played it again. And then again. Each time singing as hard as he could. After the third rendition, he allowed the disk to move on to Fleetwood Mac and he turned the volume down. And then he wiped the tear tracks from his face. Fuck, he was a mess. It was getting better, but man this still sucked. He looked at his watch. He only had a couple of hours before it got dark

If he was going to go for a run, he had better get a move on. He went into his bedroom to change into running gear.

As he came out of the bedroom, Gunner, his German short-haired pointer, noted the change in attire. The dog quivered from head to foot. He bent down and put the choke chain around his neck. As he stood up, Gunner headed towards the door. The phone rang. He turned towards the phone just as Gunner took up the slack in the leash. The sharp and sudden tug caught him off balance and he fell to the carpeted floor. Gunner came back and licked his face to apologize. He struggled to his feet and picked up the phone before it got to the fourth ring.

19

"Hello," was his greeting.

"Is this the Cop?" asked a smooth, feminine voice.

A smile crossed his lips. And then it turned into a shit-eating grin.

"Who's asking?" was his retort.

"Peacekeeper," was the answer.

"Then, yeah, this is the Cop," was all that he could think of to say.

Silence enveloped the phone line. Again, since he didn't know what to say, he didn't say anything. After an awkward ten seconds, he realized that this was not going anywhere. So, he uttered the only thing that came to his mind, "You asked me to call so I did."

There was more silence, but the duration was shorter. And then she asked, "Why, Mr. Cop, did you call me when you are wearing a wedding ring?"

He relaxed just a bit and let out a slight chuckle. "Well, Ms. Peacekeeper, I called because you asked me to, and I was wearing my ring when you did so. If you want to know why I wear this ring, I'll tell you, but not over the phone," he answered.

"That's a pretty unusual pick-up line," she responded. "When do you plan on telling me this tale?"

"I was just about to go for a run when you called. What are you doing now? How about I meet you somewhere and we can go for a walk before I run?" His own response surprised him even as it came out of his mouth. He couldn't remember being so bold.

There was a pause on the other end of the line. He thought he could hear her thinking. And then she responded, "OK, I'll meet you for a run. How long will it take you to get to the entrance to the Community Forest behind the dorms?"

He knew the place well. It was about two miles from his house.

"Twenty minutes," he said.

"Twenty minutes it is," and the phone line went dead.

He looked at Gunner and stated, "What the hell have I gotten myself into now." Gunner looked at him with cocked head and then started to tug on the leash. He headed out the door and realized that the shit-eating grin was back. He eased into a steady jog as he got to the street, but Gunner wanted to run and pulled on the lead. He upped the pace just a bit. He didn't want to be winded when he got to campus, but he agreed with his dog; he didn't want to be late either.

His gait ate up the ground and as he turned onto the road that ran through the dorms and continued on into the forest, he saw another runner in front of him. He could tell that it was a woman from her shape, but she was wearing a beanie and her hair wasn't visible. He wondered. And then as if on cue, she stopped and turned to face him. His grin returned, for it was her, the Peacekeeper. She wore knee high wool socks, running shorts, a purple sweatshirt, and a multi-colored beanie that looked like it belonged on Bob Marley's head. Sure enough, he could see that her hair was coiled underneath the hat. He stopped in front of her. Gunner, mostly because he didn't have a lot of choice, stopped too. He looked into her eyes, while Gunner sniffed her feet and then moved up her legs. She reached down and pet his head. He kept on sniffing. She smiled while she patted the dog's head, but when her eyes returned their focus to him, they were devoid of emotion.

"Do you want to walk and talk now, or do you want to wait until we get to the climb? I won't be able to run and talk at the same time," he asked her. She didn't say anything but turned and started running. He and Gunner followed. He admired the way the muscles in her legs moved. She was graceful, there was no doubt about it. He thought about his own running style. While he was a competent runner, he was anything but graceful and far from fast. More like a bull crashing through a china shop. But he liked to run, liked the way it made him feel, and he liked that he could cry openly, and no one would notice, thinking it was sweat running down his face. And it was time that he got to spend with Gunner, the one friend that wouldn't let him down and loved him no matter what he did.

The road they were on entered the trees and started to climb along a small creek. He pulled alongside her, but they didn't speak, not a word. He took occasional glances at her and he thought that she was doing the same as they ran at the same time alone and together. The road narrowed to a trail and they had to close to stay side by side. He let Gunner off his lead and allowed him to run ahead to make more room. Even so, their arms occasionally brushed. He felt a bit of an electric shock each time it happened. They got to a small earthen dam and the road forked on the top. She turned to the right, but as the trail began a steep climb, she slowed to a walk. He put Gunner back on his leash and walked alongside her. She wasn't breathing hard. He took a couple of deep breaths to try and get his composure back.

"Talk," was all she said.

"You want to know about my wedding ring?" he asked as he looked at his ring finger and twisted the simple gold band. He turned to look at her, expecting some verbal affirmation, but all he saw was a deadpan look that told him that was exactly what she wanted him to talk about.

So, he dove right in, "I was married until about ten months ago, December 18th, to be exact."

But before he could continue, she interrupted him with just a slight hint of anger in her voice, "So you got divorced and can't let go?"

"No, that's not it," he responded with just as much if not more anger in his voice. "My wife was playing stupid car games with a friend and crashed her car into a tree. The tree crushed her skull. That's why I'm not married anymore, but I still wear my ring." He had turned away from her as he uttered these words. He looked back and saw that her facial features had changed. They had softened. He saw sorrow and maybe a bit of concern. And those blue eyes were bright and looking at him.

He heard her say the words, "I'm sorry."

Before he could stop himself, he answered with the retort that had become second nature to him when he heard these words, "Why, did you kill her?" He was looking at her when he said this and he could see her face change once again. It wasn't soft anymore, more a combination of confusion and anger. He immediately realized what an asshole he was being and apologized, "I'm sorry, that was uncalled for. I don't think you would understand, but I am very tired of those words and so I lash out when I hear them."

They walked in an awkward silence for another minute. Gunner was impatient and wanted to run, but he held the lead tight. He knew he had fucked up, but he wasn't ready to give up just yet. Not now and not with this woman. He stole a glance at her but could not get a read on what she was thinking. Her eyes appeared to be hidden by storm clouds. They walked on, both holding their thoughts tight, not wanting to be the first to speak. And then they both turned towards each other and stated simultaneously, "Let's start over." They both laughed just a little, a laugh at the release of so much tension. They stopped walking when Gunner sniffed at an interesting azalea bush. They turned to face each other. Their eyes found each other. And he felt himself get lost in those blue irises, a blue the color of the alpine sky on a clear day. He stared, feeling awkward about not breaking his gaze. But he saw that she was doing the same thing and he widened his focus. The look on her face was stunningly beautiful. He saw kindness, desire, longing, affection and who knows what else. He had seen a lot of looks in his time; he thought he was pretty good at reading expressions, but he could not recall a woman looking at him this way. Not even his wife had looked at him like that.

And so he said the first thing that came to his mind, "You're stunningly beautiful."

Her response surprised him, although he didn't know why. All she said was, "Thank you for noticing."

No more words were spoken; they stayed close in comfortable silence, and they may have remained that way, but Gunner's patience, and he was a pretty patient dog, was at an end. He barked once and tugged at the leash. Regretfully, he looked at his dog and scratched him between his ears.

"I have to get my miles in. Would you like to run with me?" he asked. But he could see the answer before he heard the words.

"No, I have to get to class," were the words when they came out. But he could also see that this was true and not that she was blowing him off. And to confirm this, she followed up with, "What are you doing tomorrow?"

"I have to work from 3:00 to 11:00 tomorrow night," was his answer.

"I have class in the morning, but I have to work the dinner shift tomorrow night. Why don't you swing by the restaurant when you get off work and I'll wait for you?" was the response he got.

"I can't be sure that I will get off on time. Things happen and I often have to work late. How will I contact you if I am late or can't make it?" he asked.

"Well, just make sure that "things" don't happen. I'll wait for you until midnight. I have some reading to do," was her answer.

Their eyes locked once again. He knew he had to go, but he sure didn't want to. So, he asked, "Can I give you a hug?"

She responded by wrapping her arms around his neck and pulling him close. He, in turn, wrapped his arms around her back and squeezed gently. He felt the warmth of her body, her breasts against his chest, and the rush of blood towards his groin. Before he embarrassed himself, he broke the hug and gave her a gentle kiss on the cheek. He whispered, "Thank you" in her ear and took a half step back. Her head cocked to the side, much like Gunner did when he didn't understand. So, he repeated, "Just thank you." And with that he turned and started to run up the hill. He didn't look back, but Gunner did. And he gave out a quick double bark and took off up the hill as fast as he could pull his human. For the dog had seen the look on both the woman's and his human's faces and he knew that the times were a changing. He was glad to see his human smile, but was a bit nervous about keeping his spot on the waterbed in the future.

Chapter Four

Big City

October 26, 1996, 2345 Hours

He looked at his watch. 11:45. Shit, he was late and getting later. He was supposed to have gotten off of work 45 minutes ago. He heard Raymond softly snoring in the backseat. It would be hours before he was done for the night, and he just hoped that he could get to the restaurant before she left. His mind rewound to a few hours earlier.

It had been a quiet shift, so it looked like he was going to be able to get off on time and meet the Peacekeeper as planned. And then the call came out:

"A15, Dispatch, report of an escalating verbal 415 at 1956 Main Street."

"A15, roger."

"A15, Dispatch, neighbor reports that she can hear something repeatedly hitting the wall and a woman screaming."

"A15, roger."

He knew the place, knew the apartment, knew the people. Raymond was a family man, hardworking, loving to his wife and family. Until he started to drink that is. Then he became a raging asshole that beat the shit out of everyone in his path. He would apologize and try to make up in the morning. But until then... he flipped on the car's rotating lights and accelerated.

"Dispatch, A15, I'm out on Main."

"A15 is out at 1956 Main, assault in progress. Second unit is en route from Big City, Code-3, ETA is ten minutes."

"A15 copies."

He parked on the wrong side of the street, a house and a half away from Raymond's apartment complex. He approached as quickly as he could while still being quiet. He eased up the stairs and paused just to the right of the door to Raymond's apartment where he could hear a woman sobbing. As he reached for the door, it opened. A boy of about six stood in the entry. His face was blank.

"Jose, where's your dad?" he whispered.

The boy turned around halfway and pointed towards a bedroom door.

Again, a whisper. "Is your mom ok?"

Jose pointed towards the kitchen. Elena was sitting at the kitchen table, her head in her hands. There was blood on her face, and it was dripping slowly onto the table. He keyed the mic on his radio and spoke softly:

"Dispatch, A15, request medical for a 36-year-old assault victim, breathing and conscious. She has unknown head injuries. Request medical stage at the gas station."

"Dispatch copies, medical to stage at 1800 Main for an assault victim." The response seemed overly loud in the quiet room. He turned down the volume on his radio, thinking better late than never.

He moved past Jose and into the kitchen. Elena did not move. They had been down this road together more than once. There was a red welt above her eye. The blood was coming from her nose. And there was more blood in her hair.

"Elena are you ok?" he said still whispering.

"Sí."

As he started to move towards the bedroom, he could hear her start to cry again. As he approached the door, he could hear a new sound: rhythmic, steady and getting louder. He opened the door slowly. Raymond lay on the bed fully, clothed. His snores filled the room. He eased into the room quietly. He had a handcuff on one hand before Raymond even woke up. A bit of twisting pressure and the other arm was secured. Raymond's eyes blinked as he tried to comprehend what had just happened. And then he put his head back down and resumed snoring.

"Dispatch, A15, Code-4, one in custody. You can cancel the second unit and have medical come in."

"Roger, A15 is Code-4 with one in custody."

The rest of the call seemed to take forever. He photographed Elena's injuries, the blood in the kitchen, the holes in the living room sheetrock made by the back of her head, and the overturned coffee table. He had put Raymond in the back seat of his patrol car and when he checked on him, he was sound asleep. The firemen arrived and took Elena's vitals and the paramedic from the ambulance crew checked her for a concussion. But he knew she wasn't going anywhere. She had refused medical treatment every time before. The medical first responders all got back in their trucks and headed for home. He told Elena that he would come back and check on her the next day. Then

29

he drove Raymond to the police station. More photographs, some paperwork, and off to the jail in the Big City. And here he was forty-five minutes late and he still had more than a mile to go.

Raymond awoke as he slowed and turned into the restaurant parking lot. "Hey boss, you going to buy me dinner?" he asked.

"Do us both a favor and go back to sleep," was his response. "And my name is Mark."

"Whatever you say boss," was the snide comment from the backseat.

And there she was. The dome light in the Toyota was on and he could see her face framed by her hair. She appeared to be concentrating on the book propped against the steering wheel. As his headlights played across the truck, she looked up and saw his police car. She turned off the dome light and got out as he came to a stop.

"You're late," was all she said.

"I had a call right before the end of my shift. I have to take my friend here to the jail and then go back to work and get my report done. I won't get off until the wee hours of the morning," was his response. Raymond was snoring in the backseat again.

She answered, "I have a test in the morning, and I am going to be up all-night studying. Would you like to watch the sun come up with me?"

He was a bit speechless; he didn't know what to say. Raymond stopped snoring. "Hey, pussy!" erupted from the backseat as Raymond found his voice.

"Hey! Shut up and I'll buy you a burger before we get to the jail." He turned to address the girl, but before he could speak.

"Fries too, boss?"

"Yes, fries too. Now go back to sleep so that I can talk with this young lady," he pleaded.

He turned and looked at her. She had that smile on her face again. He lowered his voice and asked, "I'd love to meet you, but where?"

"I like to listen to the sound of the waves on the beach while I study. How about the parking lot across from the power plant on the North Jetty? The one with the monument," was her answer.

He knew the area a bit. "Ok, I'll meet you there after I get done with work. See you in a couple of hours." He watched her get back in her truck, smile at him in the darkness and then she was gone, her headlights lighting up the darkness as she pulled away.

As he got back in his patrol car, Raymond's slurred speech once again came from the backseat. "Jefe, that's some mighty fine pussy. What does she see in you? You're uglier than a cow's face."

He wondered the same thing as he left the parking lot and pulled into the late-night drive-through of the burger place down the street. He didn't know. He was quite a few years older then her. Maybe more than quite a few. But he bought a burger, fries, and a Coke for Raymond and then approached the sally-port entrance to the jail. He pushed the button on the talk box and when prompted, responded with, "Small Town PD with one male, cooperative." The doors opened and he drove into the jail. He pretended to complete his booking paperwork while Raymond ate. And so began another day; a day that he would not forget anytime soon.

Chapter Five

The Beach

October 28, 1996, 0358 Hours

He pulled into the parking area at about four in the morning. Her truck was there, the only vehicle in sight. He grabbed the thermos he had brought. Her truck was dark, and he used his flashlight to make sure she wasn't in it. He looked towards the water and he could see a glow coming from behind a large piece of driftwood, a root-wad with part of the trunk still attached. He walked that way, through the soft sand, not thinking that he was going to have to polish his boots before he went back to work. The air was calm, but the night was cool, as was the norm in late Fall. The waves beat a steady tempo on the shore, but he could detect no other sound. He didn't know what to expect. He thought briefly about the possibility that he was approaching someone else in the wee hours of the morning, but he walked on and as he rounded the end of the log, his apprehensions both eased and intensified. She was there, lit by a lantern, her back against the wood, focusing on the book in her lap. He stopped briefly, intent on trying to soak up as much of the moment as he could before he moved on. Blonde hair cascading from beneath a beanie, a wine red blanket pulled up to her chest, a homespun sweater covering her arms, and a scarf of many colors wrapped around her neck. There was the faint odor of burned marijuana in the air. He watched her, a second, maybe two. Well, maybe longer. He was fascinated by the shadow created by the lantern light and the way it moved as the flame danced. His forward momentum had ceased entirely. Then the book lowered slowly, and her head turned to look at him.

His ears heard, "Quit gawking and come sit by me. I'm starting to get cold."

He started to move again, his feet in the proper direction, his hands opening the thermos. He knelt down beside her and poured the fluid into a cup.

"It's hot chocolate. I didn't know if you drank coffee or not, much less how you like it, so I thought this would be safer. But at least it is still warm."

He watched her hands reach out to take the cup. They were encased in wool mittens. Steam rose into the night air and the faint scent of chocolate mixed with the marijuana to create a smell he kind of liked. He watched her eyes as she lifted the cup to her lips. There was the hint of a smile there. And then they turned towards him and they locked. It was too dark to see all the details, but he thought he could see both contentment and thanks in her face. He wondered what he was projecting. He hoped it wasn't too lustful. Even so, he broke the silence, nervous that his face might betray his uncertainty.

"I have a sleeping bag in my car if you're cold, but I am afraid it would clash with all your natural fibers."

Her response was to lift the corner of the blanket. "Come sit with me, we'll be fine together."

He lifted the blanket and crawled under it. He found that she had placed a foam pad against the log and there was another blanket between him and the sand. Not knowing just what to expect, he left a small gap between them as he pulled the top blanket up and covered himself. In the meantime, she had closed her book, finished the cocoa, and turned off the lantern. When she rolled back towards him, he noticed that the gap he had left was gone. He had no idea if this was intentional or not. His next thought was that he thought too much.

And, as she often did, she sensed his slight discomfort and took the lead. Her left hand found his right as she laid her head on his shoulder. He could feel the warmth of her body despite all the wool layers between them.

"I'm tired," she whispered. "Talk to me until I fall asleep."

"What do you want me to talk about?" he countered.

"Start at the beginning," was her simple reply.

So, he started at the beginning, telling her of growing up in Southern California and of his family's cabin in the mountains. He described the pleasure he received from listening to the wind move through the trees, the smell of pines, and the bite of cold air on bare skin. How his time in the forest, so different from the one here, had caused him to study forestry so that he would always be near the woods. He felt her stir only once, as she snuggled closer and changed the position of her head. But he was overcome by her smell. It was an exotic combination of shampoo and marijuana, with just a hint of an unwashed body and wool. But there was something else too. He didn't recognize it, but it made him think of damp earth. He struggled briefly telling her about coming to Big Tree County, about his time working in the woods, not to save them as was her intention, but to harvest them.

But she settled this issue too, as her breathing became audible in the still, night air. It was slow, steady, and rhythmic, the breathing of sound sleep.

He soaked it in. He felt a warmth throughout his being. It felt good to be alive. And he realized that he hadn't felt this way since Karen died. He smiled, at first just a bit of a grin. But he couldn't help himself and the grin grew until it covered his entire face. He listened to the sound of the waves as his own eyelids grew heavy. He fought the sensation as he wanted to enjoy this feeling for as long as he could. But it had been a long day and before he could register a complaint, consciousness faded.

He awoke to sunlight and found that he was alone. He was a bit chilled despite still being wrapped in the blankets. He stood and looked around. The sun was still low on the horizon, but at this time of year, he thought it must be mid-morning. Her truck was gone. So too, was the lantern, her book, and his thermos. But there was still a faint whiff of her scent on the blanket. He smiled again as he shook the sand from the heavy blankets and folded them into squares. He carried them back to his car. And there pinned under the windshield wiper was a sheet of paper, damp with the dew. He unfolded it carefully and discovered that she had left him a note written in pencil.

Mark,

Sorry I had to leave you, but it was time for class. You missed the sunrise. Thank you for the hot chocolate. Please bring the blankets with you to dinner, my place at about six. You can bring dessert if you like.

P.K.

PS – Your snoring is kind of sexy.

He buried his nose into the blanket, seeking her scent. And finding just a trace of it, he surprised himself by beginning to cry. Not sobs, just little drops forming at the corners of his eyes and making a slow trek down his cheek until they were absorbed by the coarse wool.

"Lord, what a mess I am," he said to himself. But he knew he was lying. He wasn't a mess. He was starting to feel alive again and it felt good. Again, the warmth flooded through his core. But it wasn't reaching his skin, so he put the blankets in the trunk, climbed into the car, and turned the heater up.

As he headed down the road towards home, he turned on the radio. A sultry voice was trying to sell him a used car. But when the commercial ended, he heard the synthesizers of the Eurhythmics' *Here Comes the Rain Again*. As Annie Lennox started to sing, he joined in:

Here comes the rain again
Falling on my head like a memory
Falling on my head like a new emotion
I want to walk in the open wind
I want to talk like lovers do
I want to dive into your ocean
Is it raining with you
So baby talk to me
Like lovers do
Walk with me
Like lovers do
Talk to me
Like lovers do

As the first chorus ended he thought, *man am I getting ahead of myself.* But regardless of what the future might bring, he felt wanted again, the one thing he had missed the most. And so, he sang on, even as he had to turn on the windshield wipers to clear away the first windborne rain drops.

Chapter Six

College Town

October 28, 1996, 1748 Hours

He drove up the hill, winding his way through the second growth redwoods. He admitted to himself that he had butterflies in his stomach. It was kind of like at the kickoff of a rugby game. Back then, as soon as he took or made the first hit, the feeling was gone. He hoped that would be the case tonight, but this was so different than a mere game. Or was it? What was he looking for out of this thing? It had been sweet and, in some ways, beautiful, but was it going to last? He decided maybe he had better pay more attention to the road. He slowed, looking at the numbers that had been placed on the occasional mailbox or post. The road turned and through a break in the trees he could look to the west. The sun had just set, but there was still a rosy glow on the scattered clouds leftover from the morning's squall. There was a wide spot in the road, and he pulled in to watch the colors fade. He got out of his car and sat on the hood. He could see the lights of College Town below and further west, the faint white lines as the waves crashed onto the shore.

His sleeping spot from the morning was obscured by trees, but it caused him to relive the warmth he had felt. As the warmth spread, it clashed with the queasiness in his stomach. The butterflies retreated and he felt just a bit of confidence. And he felt then that this was more than a game. This was life and he was going to live it. He got back in his car.

The road made a sharp switchback just past the turnout where he had stopped and as he settled into a northward climb, his headlights picked up the numbers he was looking for next to a driveway. He slowed, looking for a place to park. Sure enough, on the opposite side of the road was a turnout large enough for his car. He pulled in, parked, and gently eased the box containing the chocolate raspberry cheesecake out of the backseat, where he had used the seatbelt to keep it from sliding around. He had spent most of the afternoon working on it and he didn't want it to end up on the floorboards, upside down. He had made this dessert once before and it had turned out better than he had hoped. He prayed that would be the case again. He still had most of a bottle of framboise, a raspberry liquor, that was essential for the sauce he would pour over each slice. It had been hard to find in this isolated community and he was glad that he didn't have to search for it again. But everything else he had easily found at his neighborhood market on his way home from the beach; Oreos for the crust (and maybe one or two to eat while he was baking), fresh raspberries, cream, good chocolate, and cream cheese. It had good stuff in it and he had learned that if you use good ingredients, the concoction usually turned out pretty good too, although it was rarely easy on your waist.

He walked down the dirt driveway and came to a large house. It was dark, however, and it didn't look like anyone was home. For just a second, he wondered what was going on, but then a light came on and he saw a well-trodden path that went around the south side of the house. He went that way and as he rounded the corner of the garage, he saw that there was a cabin behind the house, tucked into a small grove of trees. The lights in the cabin were on and there was just a bit of smoke coming from the stove pipe above the roof. He paused briefly before proceeding. The cabin was small, probably only about five hundred square feet. But as he took in his surroundings, he realized that he was standing in a small opening in the forest and that the view from the large windows would encompass College Town and the ocean beyond. As he got closer to the front door, he realized that the view also included the turnout where he had stopped only a few minutes before. Had she seen him gathering his courage? Had she known what he was doing? Before he could dwell on this further, the door opened and there she was.

Her head was tilted slightly to one side as if asking a question. Her hair flowed freely, framing her face, which was formed into a half-smile; a smile that was also asking questions. Large earrings dangled and flashed as they caught the light. As he got closer, he could see that they were made in part of abalone shells. A multihued, but mostly blue, orb with black and white flecks, about the size of a marble, hung on a leather lace around her neck. He thought the colors of the pendant matched her eyes. She wore a loose, white cotton dress that ended just below her knees. The bodice had embroidery in vibrant colors, but he didn't want to spend too much attention there, so he focused on her eyes. He realized that she was doing the same. She had the advantage, as her face was in the shadow of the porch light, while his was fully lit. So, he concentrated on the smile that was slowly taking over her entire face. Her head straightened, but still not a word had been spoken. She stepped to the side and encouraged him to enter with a wave of her hand. Desire overcame inertia and his feet started to move. As he walked up the steps, she took the box from his hands and followed him inside, closing the heavy door behind her.

As he entered the house, he took in his surroundings. It was obviously a cabin that had been built for a single occupant, or maybe an intimate couple. The cabin was one large room. In one corner was a toilet, sink and a shower stall. There was a portable partition that provided just a hint of privacy. A bed occupied an adjacent corner. And as before, he elected not to focus on that location, so his eyes moved to the rest of the room. The portion next to the door was a small kitchen with a range, sink, short counters, and a refrigerator. And the far corner was occupied by a small table with three chairs. Against the wall sat a small stereo system with a turntable. A second door was on the far wall and a wood stove stood near the center of the room. The walls were covered with knotty pine siding and there were several enlarged photographs on the walls. But what he most wanted to see was behind him, so he turned around.

She had placed his box on a kitchen counter and was watching him take a visual survey of her living quarters. Again, his eyes found hers. He realized that he wanted contact, that he wanted to touch her. He took a step in her direction, hesitated, but then continued. He placed his hands on her shoulders and she did not flinch. He slid his hands down her back and tried to pull her gently towards him in a simple hug. He felt a bit of tension in her body, and found her arms between them. He started to pull back, but before he could disengage completely, her arms slid out from between them and she moved into the hug, her head resting on his chest and her arms encircling his back. His brief apprehension eased, and he gathered her in. His senses were overwhelmed, the smell of her hair in his nostrils, the feeling of her breasts against his chest, the sound of her breathing. He closed his eyes, and the warmth filled the core of his being one more time. He held the hug; he didn't want to let go. But he could feel her start to stir and so he shifted his weight backwards and away from her. He opened his eyes and was treated to the eyes and to the smile, the combination which had captivated him so. They stood together, his hands on her shoulders, hers resting on his waist. Their eyes were locked together once more. As far as he was concerned, they could spend the rest of the night in this position.

But again, she stirred and then she turned back to her kitchen. He followed and watched her as she stirred a pot of boiling water. A second burner held a large pot with a simmering red sauce. She stirred it also. He could detect hints of garlic, oregano and rosemary as the spoon moved to and fro.

She turned her head and asked, "Are you a carnivore?"

He nodded his head in the affirmative and continued to watch her as she turned back to her work. She went to the refrigerator and took out a plate that held four large, precooked meatballs. She slowly lowered each one into the sauce and then she turned down the heat.

"You don't talk much, do you?" she asked.

"I have learned that when in the presence of great beauty, it is often best to simply soak it in and try not to ruin it with words," was his reply. He heard a light chuckle and then she turned back towards him.

"How has that bullshit line worked for you in the past?" But the smile was still on her face and he could tell that she was playing with him, kind of like a cat with a toy, or maybe with a mouse, just before the kill.

"No bullshit. What could be more beautiful than a gorgeous woman making pasta? This evening's sunset can't compare." He said it with a straight face even though he knew he was pushing the limits of credibility. Words had not always been his friend. It was too easy to say the wrong ones. She turned back to her cooking, but not before giving him a questioning look. He watched as she stirred the pasta and the sauce one more time. She then opened the oven and he got a whiff of fresh baked bread. She removed a cookie sheet that had a loaf of bread covered by a towel. She removed the towel, placed the bread on a cutting board and handed him a cerated knife.

"Make yourself useful." The words were a demand, but they were spoken softly and with a smile.

He sat the knife down and moved alongside of her at the sink. He quickly washed his hands and then took up the knife once again. He held the still warm loaf so that the bottom faced him and started to cut slices. He found a large bowl in a cupboard and a clean cloth napkin in a drawer. He unfolded the napkin and laid it in the bowl so that the edges hung over the sides. The bread went on top and then he folded the edges back over the bread to keep it warm just a bit longer. He took the bowl and placed it in the middle of the table. He then found more napkins, none of which matched the others, and silverware. He quickly set the table as she continued to work the stove. A wine goblet went at one setting and a tumbler at the other. As he finished, he turned and saw that she was ladling sauce and meatballs over spaghetti. She placed one bowl at each setting. Next was a small bowl of grated parmesan cheese and then a plate with a stick of butter. When she tried to pour a red wine into his tumbler, he covered it with his hand.

"I'm sorry, but I don't drink."

"Are you an alcoholic?" was her response. It caught him a bit off guard. Most people weren't so direct. When he didn't respond right away, she added, "I have cranberry juice and water."

He went to the fridge and poured himself a glass of juice and set it down next to his plate. She was looking around the room, apparently trying to figure out if she needed to do anything else. He went to her chair and pulled it out. She tilted her head and formed the questioning smile, but she sat down. As he pushed in her chair, he lowered his head so that he could smell her hair. Once again the slightly perfumed scent of her shampoo filled his nose. There was more though, scents he couldn't identify, but the combination was captivating, and he had to force himself to stand erect before he embarrassed himself further. He sat himself and looked across the table at her. He wasn't sure what to expect next. But she smiled at him and simply said, "Bon appétit."

When her gaze shifted from him to the food in front of her, he said, "No, I'm not an alcoholic. The night my wife died… the night my wife's body was found, I had a few drinks to try and help me sleep. I didn't sleep, but when I got up the next morning, I thought that could become a terrible habit and I haven't had a drink since. I don't miss it; I never really liked the taste all that much."

He had watched her as he spoke. She had gracefully twisted the pasta onto her fork and raised it to her mouth. The pasta began to unravel before she closed her mouth. She raised her head to look at him, pursed her lips and sucked in the last strand of spaghetti, the sauce dribbling down her lips. He knew she was putting on a show, trying to lighten the mood. He didn't know if she was trying to be funny, sexual or a bit of both. But he appreciated the effort, smiled heartily, and began to eat himself.

They talked as they ate. She wanted to know what it was like to be a police officer. He wanted to know more about her, where she grew up, what she liked to do. He told her that his work as a small-town patrol officer was often far from exciting. While the same types of events occurred in his city as in larger ones, they just didn't happen as often. He could spend a day and the highlight would be arresting a vagrant dog or trying to herd a horse back to its pasture. She told him of growing up in the southern part of Big Tree County, of spending most of her day outdoors. And they both talked of the things they liked; music, movies, art, and food. Neither one said anything that wasn't true. But neither one told the whole story either. It was kind of like the opening moves in a chess game, each side hinting at meaning, feeling out the other with feinting, pawn-like words, but keeping the important pieces in reserve.

When they were done he helped her clear the table. They stood side-by-side at the sink, she washing, he rinsing and drying. They continued to talk. He learned that the house belonged to her aunt, who was not rich, but comfortable. She was spending the winter in Arizona and had just left town. The aunt let her stay in the cabin in exchange for looking after the place while she was gone. It was one of the reasons she could afford to go to school. She loved to wake up and see the morning sun reflect off the ocean below. And he told her that he shared his house with a couple of student roommates. He explained that after Karen died, he couldn't afford to live there alone, and he felt that the company was good for him, that it kept him from dwelling too much on the past. He didn't mention that it also kept him from being alone all the time.

"Thank you for helping with the dishes. I hope you enjoyed dinner. Did you bring the blankets with you?

"I wanted to wash them, but I was afraid that they wouldn't dry. So, I took them into the garage and shook them out as best I could. They still have a little sand on them though. They're in the trunk, I'll go get them."

He wound his way around the house and located his car in the dark. He grabbed the blankets and retraced his route. When he opened the cabin door he didn't see her inside. Instead, the door on the back wall was open, so he went that way. It was dark on this side of the place and he could see her only because she was starting a fire and she was silhouetted by the faint light. As the fire grew in size, he realized that he was on a small deck with a raised rock fire pit in the center. There were benches around the edge of the deck railing. The fire popped and crackled as the dry kindling caught. He watched her work. She had covered her dress with the wool sweater from the previous night, as the air was cool, bordering on cold. The clouds had moved on and the night sky was covered with millions of stars. When she was satisfied with the fire, she took two pillows and placed them on the bench and then covered them with one of the blankets. She encouraged him to sit and then joined him, pulling up the second blanket to their chests. She sat quietly for a minute, then got up and went back to the cabin, turning off all of the lights. She joined him once again in the cocoon of blankets and pillows. He felt as her right hand searched and found his left. She grasped it in a soft embrace. He liked the feeling, the joining sensation that it implied. He could feel the warmth of her body next to his, and it caused his groin to stir. But he forced those thoughts away as he didn't want to ruin the moment. They sat in an easy silence, both content to watch the fire and the stars. The wind played through the trees and created a harmony with the patter of the fire. He didn't think things could get any better. And then they did.

She raised his arm and slid in underneath it so that her shoulder was tucked into his armpit and her head rested on his breast. She tucked her feet up under her with her knees pointed towards the fire. She rearranged the blanket to make sure that her feet were covered and then found his right hand with hers. Once again, their fingers intertwined. His left arm fell along her torso and he rested it there after making sure she was covered.

"You like holding hands don't you," he murmured as a statement rather than a question.

"I do," was her equally soft response. "But it has a second purpose. I think I am pretty good at reading people, and you didn't seem like the type, but I have found that it helps reduce the risk of octopus arms."

"Octopus arms?" he questioned.

"Guys, who just want to grab and grope, who want to reach the destination without enjoying the journey. They have octopus arms," she clarified.

"And you think I might be that kind of guy?"

"No, I just like holding your hand. You're kind of the exact opposite, the driver who takes the scenic route not worrying about how long the journey will last. I like that kind of man. It makes the end all that much more rewarding."

He couldn't see her face, but he was confident that she was smiling. She stirred gently, rearranging the way she was draped across him.

She spoke again, "I'm sorry to do this, but I didn't get any sleep today and I am afraid that I am going to fade out again soon. We did talk today, but not about anything important. Tell me something important before I fall asleep."

Peacekeepers

He thought briefly. He liked her directness and so he thought he would reciprocate. He spoke slowly, searching his mind for the right words. "When my wife died, the world I had known crashed down around me. I lost my partner, my lover, my friend. My hopes and plans for the future were dashed. I realized that I had to start over, that I had to deal with my baggage and move on. But this has been hard. I have been a loner most of my life, an introvert. Many of the highlights of my life, I have done by myself. But I'm not a hermit. I still need to feel a connection with another person. I want to love, and I want to feel loved and needed in return. I don't want to live alone. I want to share the joys of my life with someone else, someone special."

She didn't stir, but he could tell she was still awake. So, he continued, "This morning, on the beach, that was pretty special for me. I don't think you can understand. Not until you have been where I have. It was a shared moment, simple affection with another person. And it didn't hurt that the woman who held my hand was beautiful and different from me. It warmed me to my soul. When I woke and found you gone, I cried. Not from sorrow, but from joy that I was beginning to come back to life, that perhaps the darkness, which I thought would drown me, might be coming to an end."

She still didn't stir, but he could tell from her silence that she wanted him to continue. So he did, "When I was driving home, *Here Comes the Rain Again* was playing on the radio. I have found that singing helps me deal with the anguish of grief. So, I sang. Gunner will attest that I can't sing for shit, but that's not what's important. It's the outpouring of sentiment that counts. So when I sang 'I want to talk like lovers do,' I had the feeling that it was a possibility now, where before, it was only a fantasy."

"So, you want to be lovers, to make love? You don't seem to be moving very fast in that direction," were her first words. But she didn't move when she said them, there was no reproach in her voice. And he detected a suggestion that making love was not out of the realm of possibility. He paused, gathering his thoughts into something that he hoped would be coherent.

"I have enjoyed sex. I have missed it. But what I miss more is the feeling of companionship, of the feeling of belonging to something greater than myself. Sex, or the lack of it, has fucked up more relationships, pun intended, than anything else. Only money, or the lack of it, comes close. I don't want to lose what we have found here. I have been as honest as I can be. I am counting on you to guide me further, to tell me what you want from me."

She twisted in his arms as he finished speaking. She was facing him now, their faces separated only by inches. "You are a beautiful man, wounded, but beautiful." She gave him a quick kiss on the lips, and before he could respond, she had her feet on the deck and was helping him up.

"You're as tired as I am, I can tell. Come with me," she directed and led him into the dark of the cabin. The fire was left to sputter within its rock walls and the blankets, he realized as he followed her into the cabin, to collect the morning dew.

She paused inside the door and lit a candle with a lighter that was on a shelf. He saw that there was a jar of marijuana buds and rolling papers on the same shelf. He wasn't surprised. She used the candlelight to guide their path from one corner of the cabin to the other. She set the candle down on a nightstand and turned to him.

"Take off whatever clothes you are comfortable with. You can set them down on the chair."

50

He watched as she turned down the blankets before deftly pulling her dress over her head. She was wearing only a light-colored bra and panties. She then busied herself tending to the woodstove while he took off his clothes down to his underwear. He wanted to, but he couldn't look away when she bent down to add more wood to the fire and turn down the damper. He was unsure where this was heading but decided to play it out. He was conscious that his penis was erect and there was no hiding his excitement.

When she turned back to him, she made no mention of the bulge in his underwear. As far as he could tell, she hadn't even glanced down. Instead, she motioned for him to get into the bed. He did so, sliding to the far side of the double bed. She followed and pulled the covers over them both. He rested on his right side facing her. She rolled onto her right side also and snuggled up against him, her rear end pushing against his groin. But again, there were no words. It was as if his hardness was to be expected. Her left hand found his and she pulled his arm across her belly, just below her breasts.

"I like the scenic route," was all she said as she blew out the candle.

He awoke once in the night to the sound of rain on the cabin's metal roof. He could still feel her next to him, her breathing slow and steady. His one conscious thought before falling back into a deep sleep was *it was a good night to be alive.*

When he awoke again, there was sun beaming though a skylight. His nostrils recognized the smell of bacon. He raised himself up and looked in the kitchen. She was standing in profile, working at the range. Her hair was wrapped in a towel and she was wearing a bathrobe, and the abalone earrings still dangled and caught the light. He couldn't turn away. He wanted to behold this sight for as long as possible. His attention caught hers, however, and she turned to look at him, a smile forming on her lips.

"Good morning sleepy-head."

"Good morning sunshine," was his response. And it seemed to fit as a cloud must have passed overhead as new rays of light found their way through the skylight and onto her face.

"I don't have much time this morning. I have to get dressed and go to work. Get up and come eat while I get ready for work." She removed the towel from her head and wet hair cascaded down once again. He watched her from the bed as stood in front of a mirror between the bed and the bathroom and ran a brush through her tresses. He couldn't remember the last time he had seen someone do this. And without thinking, without speaking, he climbed out of bed and stood behind her. He could see her smile in the mirror. He gently took the brush from her hand and began to run it through her long straight locks. He was gentle and slow. He couldn't describe the feeling. It was sensual, magical, and just a bit erotic all mixed into the slow, steady strokes of the brush. Again, it was something that he thought he could do forever, but alas it was not to be. She turned to face him, gave him another quick kiss on the lips, and then took back her brush.

"Go eat, I have to get dressed and go."

Reluctantly, he turned, pulled on his shirt from the night before and stepped into his pants. As the blood that had been rushing through his body began to slow, he realized that the floor was rather cold, and he found his socks. He made the short walk to the kitchen and found a plate with scrambled eggs, toast, and a couple of strips of bacon. He picked up the plate and carried it to the table. He sat himself, took a bite, and only then, did he focus his attention to the other side of the room. His timing was near perfect as she was zipping up the short skirt she needed to wear for work while still facing the mirror. He watched her as he chewed. She ran the brush through her hair a couple more times, flicked her bangs to the side, tucked one side behind her ear, and then shook her head, undoing all of the little gestures in one swoop. She turned around and caught him starring at her again as she sat on the bed to put on her shoes.

"Eat your breakfast before it gets cold," she demanded. "I'm done putting on a show."

He wondered if she thought he had watched her the whole time she was getting dressed. But she was smiling now, and he realized that maybe it didn't really matter all that much. She seemed to be very comfortable in her own skin.

"When will I see you again?" he asked.

"I have to work, and I have more midterms that I need to study for. It might be a few days. But I have something in mind, something that I thought of when you told me about driving home from the beach this morning. I just have to wait for the right conditions. I'll call you. In the meantime, why don't you write me a letter? I left you my box number on the table."

She took a coat from a hook by the door, shrugged her way into it, and gave him another peck, this time on the cheek. "Your cheesecake was really good. I had a piece for breakfast. Leave me a slice when you go."

And then the door closed, and he was alone. But the warmth was still there inside of him, even as he chewed cold eggs and bacon.

Chapter Seven

Small Town

October 29, 1996, 1710 Hours

He walked through the back door of the station just as the sun was going down behind him. He was early for his graveyard shift, which didn't start for several hours. His mind was still on the feel of the girl next to him as she slept. He had decided maybe he needed some extra time to get his mind into work mode tonight. So here he was. As he passed through the quiet squad room, he found his friend, Bill, eating a sandwich and reading a paperback at the large table in the meeting room.

"Working hard as usual, I see. "

"What the fuck are you doing here so early," was Bill's response. "What's with the shit-eating grin?" There was a short, wordless pause while they continued to look at each other. "Oh, shit, don't tell me you got laid?"

"No." But he could tell that his face still wore a huge smile and after a few more moments of silence, he added, "But I did have a pretty amazing weekend." Amazing didn't seem to do the time they had spent together justice.

"The girl from the protest?"

"Yeah, we spent some time together, at the beach and then at her cabin on Tipton Hill. She's a pretty amazing cook and a good listener."

"Listener? Don't tell me you talked her to death." He could tell that Bill was teasing him, but he also realized that this was his way of asking for more without pressing. He was a good friend; he had helped him through some of the worst of times, but he wasn't sure that he wanted to tell him what had happened, how they had slept together twice, but had not even really kissed. He didn't think, good friend or not, that he would understand.

"She wants me to write her a letter."

"Well, that's a step in the right direction. Up to now, you were writing love letters and the only person reading them was me," his tone changing from jocular to warm. "You do write a pretty good letter. Who knows, you just might get laid."

He decided to change the subject. "Anything going on tonight?"

"There's going to be a party at the bar tonight. There are some bikers there now and supposedly more to come. But so far, it has been pretty quiet. Hope it stays that way." As his friend made the last utterance, he rapped himself on the head a couple of times.

"Knock on wood," was Mark's reply. "I sure hope that you didn't jinx us again."

He put on his gear for the night's shift. His Kevlar vest went over his white T-shirt. He fastened his badge to the clean uniform shirt he had brought and slipped the shirt on over his vest, tucking the tails into his pants. He cinched up the inner belt and then slipped his duty belt around his waist. He had a fully loaded Glock pistol, two additional magazines for it, two pairs of handcuffs, a can of pepper spray, a pouch filled with latex gloves, a holder for his radio, an expandable side-handle baton, and a holder for his keys. When he got the duty belt adjusted right, he tied the two belts together with leather keepers, using a double keeper at the rear so it didn't come unsnapped when he got in and out of the car seat where he would spend most of the night. He grabbed his rechargeable flashlight from the charger on the wall and slid it into the "sap" pocket on the left side of his pants. He added a pair of ballpoint pens and a small notebook to his shirt pocket, as well as a penlight and a pupil gauge. He guessed that all of the gear together must weigh at least thirty pounds. He grabbed his raincoat and went back to the meeting room.

"Ready to crush crime and suppress evil?" he asked Bill who was finishing his sandwich.

His friend got up and they walked out the back door to the waiting patrol car. He liked spending time with Bill this way. They could talk. But there was more to it than that. The shared experiences, some of them a bit harrowing, most simply mundane, brought them closer together. The camaraderie of the job was what made it worth the low pay, long hours, ugly sights, and incompetent supervisors. Well, there was also the fact that he got to carry a gun and drive fast.

Bill stashed his patrol bag, that had been occupying the passenger seat in the trunk, while Mark checked the shotgun held upright in a rack between the seats. The chamber was empty, the hammer was down, and there were four rounds of buckshot in the magazine. The sidesaddle ammo carrier attached to the receiver held four more rounds of buckshot and two slugs. He put the gun back in the rack and made his bulk comfortable in the aging Crown Victoria that was Bill's patrol car.

His friend grabbed the radio microphone and uttered, "A13 is doubled with A15 as A13."

Dispatch responded, "Roger, A13 is a double unit with A15."

They drove in small circles; the town was only so big. They spent more time close to the main street through town but explored the residential areas too. There were several motorcycles parked at the bar, but everyone was inside and staying quiet. They drove slowly, both of them looking for things that just didn't look right. They talked about anything and nothing. Sports, girls, cars, guns, and work were all the usual fodder for conversation. And of course, there was always the gossip of what was going on in the department. It was hard to keep a secret in such a small group of people. If one learned of it, they all did.

On one of their loops down the main thoroughfare, Mark saw a man walking on the sidewalk. He had a hard time putting it to words, but the man's gait just looked stiff, almost robotic. He pointed the man out to Bill and asked him if he knew him.

"I've seen him a couple of times; I think he lives on the other side of the river. You want to stop and chat him up?"

"Yeah, if you don't mind."

Bill made a U-turn after passing the man and they both watched him as he continued to walk with the stiff gait. The man waved at them as they passed. Another U-turn had them headed back towards the man and his friend stopped the car about twenty yards in front of him. He stopped walking as they both got out of the patrol car.

"Hey man, you got a minute?" Mark asked as they got closer. The man's smile slowly sank from his face.

"Why, what did I do? I'm just walking here, minding my own business."

"I see that. Neither my friend here nor I know who you are, so we thought we would stop and say hello. Mind telling us your name?" Mark asked in a mostly friendly manner.

"My name's Joe," was all the man could stammer.

"Hello Joe, my name is Mark, and this is my partner, William." Do you have any ID on you, Joe? Mind sharing it with us?"

Joe, somewhat reluctantly, took out his wallet and handed him an ID card. Mark handed it off to his partner and asked Joe in a jocular tone, "You wanted for murder, anything like that? Maybe on probation or parole?"

The man didn't say anything, but he appeared to be getting just a bit agitated. Mark looked closer at Joe. He had open sores on his face and on his hands, which seemed to continually twitch. But what really caught his attention was the size of his pupils. They were huge, taking up most of his iris. He looked at his partner's eyes and they were about half of the size of Joe's. He removed his pupil gauge and held it up next to the man's face so that he could compare the measured circles on the gauge with the size of the man's pupils. He estimated that they were about nine millimeters in diameter, maybe ten. He started to reach for his penlight, but Joe closed his eyes and wouldn't keep them open long enough for him to check to see if they were reactive to light.

"Can I leave, man? I got things to do?" was Joe's plaintive request.

"Well, Joe, I'm thinking you might be under the influence of a controlled substance." He put heavy emphasis on the words, controlled substance. "Do you use street drugs? Used any today?"

He watched as Joe seemed to retreat into himself, becoming smaller in stature. And then he heard Bill run the man through dispatch.

"Dispatch, A13. Request a local and NCIC on last of McDonald, first of Joseph, birthday is 8/13/1969."

"Roger, A13. Joseph McDonald." The dispatcher then scolded them with "A13, your location please."

"A13 is out with one in the 300 block of Main."

"Roger, 300 block of Main. McDonald is clear local and NCIC, he's on summary probation for 488 and has another screen for 647(f). No search on either probation," was the dispatcher's reply.

"Joe, you're on probation for petty theft and drunk in public. That's not so bad, what are you so nervous about?" he asked the man.

There was no answer.

"Well, Joe, let me tell you what's going to happen next. I'm going to take your pulse. Then we're going to chat a bit more. Then I'm going to ask you to take a couple of tests. Then we'll chat a bit more. And then I will take your pulse again. You up for all that?"

"Do I have a fucking choice?" was Joe's responding quip.

"No, you don't." was his reply as he retrieved a pair of latex gloves from his belt and struggled to get his fingers inside. Once he was gloved up, he took Joe's right arm and found his radial pulse. It was racing.

"You nervous Joe?" he asked. "There's nothing unusual about it if you are."

Again, there was no response. He looked at his watch and counted Joe's heartbeats. He counted thirty-two beats in fifteen seconds. He released Joe's arm.

"Your pulse is kind of high, Joe. Are you sure that you're not nervous?" he asked again.

"Fuck you, I'm done playing your fucking games."

"Well, Joe, you don't have to cooperate. But based on what I have seen so far, I have enough to arrest you for being under the influence of a stimulant. So, you can cooperate and allow me to finish my evaluation, which might show that my initial observations were incorrect, or you can say fuck it and we'll cuff you up right now. Your choice," Mark replied.

Joe turned and started to move away from him. But Bill had anticipated just such a move and had moved to cut him off. Joe stopped and again seemed to retreat inside of himself, his body language reading submission. Bill reached out, took Joe's left hand with his right, and quickly slipped a handcuff around his wrist with his weak hand. Together they brought Joe's right hand behind his back and Bill snapped the remaining cuff around that wrist. Bill then adjusted them and double-locked them with his handcuff key.

"Joe, you're under arrest for being under the influence of a controlled substance," Mark explained.

They each took one arm and walked Joe back to their patrol car.

"A13, status check," squawked over the radio.

Bill answered, "A13 is code-4, one in custody."

"Roger A13, one in custody."

When they got him next to the car, Mark fished a paper bag out of Bill's patrol bag in the trunk and started to search Joe. He removed his hat and checked the lining. The hat went in the bag. Then he ran his hands around Joe's collar and worked his way down his torso making sure that there wasn't anything under his light coat and shirt. A simple chain around his neck went into the bag.

"You got anything on you that is going to poke me, hurt me or make me bleed?" he asked Joe as he searched him.

There was no response.

You got any weapons on you, knives, guns, bazookas?" he added.

There was still no response. Instead, Joe started to cry softly.

He started to reach into Joe's pockets. There was nothing in his coat pockets. He found a wallet in Joe's right rear pocket, but it didn't contain much of interest and it was added to the bag. In his right, front, pants pocket, he found a folding knife, which also went into the bag. He then checked the coin pocket and that's where he found what he half expected to. It was a small Ziploc bag with a quantity of a yellowish colored, clumpy, powder inside. He finished checking the remainder of Joe's pockets and then ran his hands down Joe's legs, inside and out to complete the search incident to arrest.

"Joe, you're also under arrest for possession of a controlled substance," he told Joe, even though it was apparent that he knew. Joe began to cry harder, and snot started to mingle with his tears.

"Joe, you've been to jail before, what are you so upset about?" Mark asked the man who obviously was in some distress.

"You don't give a shit about me." .

"Well, if you don't tell me what's bothering you, I can't help. What's it going to hurt?"

Joe continued to cry, but was beginning to regain some sense of control. The cop reached into the car and grabbed a tissue from between the seats and used it wipe some of the fluids from Joe's face. "Ok, Joe. What's got you so emotional?"

And then it all came out. Joe's girlfriend was pregnant with his baby. She was having real problems with morning sickness and was losing weight. Tonight, she had decided she was hungry and asked Joe to go to the store and get her some ice cream. She had been eating so little that he agreed to get it for her. Now he was going to jail and there wouldn't be anyone to take care of her. The cop listened without commenting, without telling him that a father on meth was usually worse than no father at all.

"There are some that think that I am a heartless bastard, but that's not always the case," Mark told Joe. "I am always looking for information.

You tell me something interesting that I don't already know, and I might find a way to cite you out instead of taking you to jail. But it's got to be good stuff."

"I don't understand," Joe replied.

"Who did you buy your dope from," he asked directly.

"I can't tell you that."

"So, do you want to go to jail or not?" he asked. "What can you tell me?"

"Henrietta is selling weed to the high school kids."

"You're right Joe, Henrietta is selling marijuana, including to kids, but she has been arrested for it twice and is on probation already. You're going to have to do better than that ."

Joe paused, visibly weighing his options. He finally whispered, "Do you know the last house on 4th Street before it joins Queen, the one in back?

"Yeah, I know the place. Tammy Wright lives there," he responded, his interest piqued.

"Well, I have a friend who told me that every Friday, a Mexican dude shows up and drops off between one and two ounces of speed there."

"Who's your friend who told you this?" he asked.

"I can't tell you, it's the guy that I buy from. Tammy is his source."

In and of itself, it was not the most useful piece of information. But it matched some other things that he had heard. And it sounded like he was going to have to spend some time watching the last house on 4th Street.

"Ok, Joe, here's what we are going to do. We're going to go to the station. You're going to pee in a cup for me. We're going to test your dope and then I am going to write you a ticket. Then you have a choice. We can drop you off up the highway a bit so that it looks like we took you to jail, but you are going to have to find your own way back to town. Or you can walk out the back door of the station a free man, but you might have to do some explaining on why you didn't end up at the Hilton. In the meantime, I'll buy some ice cream for your girl and make sure that she gets it. You ok with all of that?"

Joe sighed but climbed into the back seat of the car. When they were finished collecting, testing and packaging the evidence, Joe signed his citation and they put him back into the patrol car, this time without handcuffs. They drove north towards Big City without putting anything out over the radio. When they got to the intersection of the State highway that headed east, they stopped and let Joe out of the back.

"You can start walking or try and ride your thumb," he told Joe. "If anybody asks what happened, just tell them that there wasn't room at the jail, and they cut you loose once you were booked."

They returned to Small Town and stopped at the gas station. He bought a pint of Hagen Daz strawberry and a Diet Coke. The clerk commented about the strange combination, but his response about dual addictions seemed to quiet her, at least for the moment. They drove around town briefly and then headed over the river to where Joe had told them that he and his girlfriend lived. Mark got out of the car and went up the walkway. The door opened before he could knock. In front of him stood a woman, a girl really, of about twenty. She was blonde and thin except for her belly. She looked to be about four, maybe five months pregnant. She was wearing an oversized T-shirt and not much else. Tears were flowing from her eyes.

"Is Joe ok?" she asked. "How badly is he hurt?"

"Joe's fine, we just stopped to bring you the ice cream that you wanted since Joe is going to be a while getting home," he answered. "Why would you assume that Joe was hurt?" he then asked as he handed her the ice cream.

He looked inside of the small house that Joe and his girl occupied. It was not what he expected. It was tidy and clean. He could see an entertainment center in the living room behind the girl. Most meth users or "tweekers" as they were commonly called would have traded the components for dope a long time ago.

"Is Joe in some kind of trouble?" he asked.

But she didn't answer his question. Instead, she took the ice cream that he had offered and started to close the door. "Thanks," was her only comment before the door shut.

"That's interesting," he said out loud, but to no one but himself.

He returned to the patrol car. He and Bill continued to patrol until Bill's shift ended at 11:00. Nothing much was going on in town. The bikers had already left the bar and the cold weather and light rain seemed to be keeping everyone in doors. He started to write the report for Joe's arrest while Bill doffed his gear.

"Take it easy and don't do anything I would do," Bill commented as he headed out the door and back towards his wife and small family. But he popped his head back in a few moments later and told him in a more serious tone, "Write that girl a letter. You're more fun to work with when you're in a good mood." And then he was gone.

He finished the report and left it in the sergeant's inbox. He headed back out on patrol. The rain had ended, the clouds had broken, and a nearly full moon was bathing the town in a soft light. He continued to drive in small circles, but he could tell that the excitement for the night was over. And he was right. He was dispatched to an address on the north end of town where a dog was alleged to be disturbing the neighborhood with its barking. However, when he got there, the dog had apparently chased away the raccoon or other demon that it was trying to warn its human about and had gone back to sleep. The remaining radio traffic was for other officers in other jurisdictions.

The night crept on, the clouds returned. Wisps of fog flowed in the draws and ravines of the surrounding hills. As was fairly common, at about 3:00 in the morning, he headed down to the river. It was flowing quickly, and while far from full, much of the riverbar was now covered with water. He parked at a spot he had found where he could see the river clearly, but not worry about getting his car stuck in the sand. He turned off the engine and listened to the sound of the river as it flowed past his vantage point. Then the wind picked up just a bit and made the nearby alders dance to its tune. This song drowned out the quiet melody of moving water. He let his mind clear, and when he felt ready, he pictured Peacekeeper. In the past, when he had come here, he had thought of Karen or occasionally, one of his good friends. The words would come to him as his mind tried to recreate a smile; sometimes they came in phrases, sometimes in whole sentences. He had referred to this process as writing love letters in search of a recipient. But now things had changed. Now there was someone who was going to read his words, words that were intended for that person and not his dead wife or a friend who didn't realize that he was writing about her. It changed the game. He knew that words were important, that they could be powerful. He was nervous, but his confidence had been boosted by what he now thought of as his practice letters. And he pictured her as she sat next to him in front of the fire, felt the warmth of her body next to his, and heard the words as she asked if he wanted to be lovers. And the words started to form. When he sat down in front of the computer at the station an hour later, this is what he typed:

Small Town PD
October 30, 1996
3:41 AM

Hi PK,

The fog rolled in as the moon was setting this morning, so the river was only lit by the streetlamps on the freeway. Yet, there was still a milky sheen reflecting off of the moving water. A few stars were visible through the holes in the fog, and they too, would reflect off the water. An occasional truck on the freeway interrupted the quiet, but I paid them little attention. This is where I come to think, to reflect on my life. I come here often when I am working, usually at least once every night, sometimes more if I am not busy. I was here a lot tonight.

This was different though. I'm usually depressed, suffering from grief. I come here for comfort, to soak in the beauty of nature. But tonight— tonight is different. I came here to give thanks. It feels good to be alive again. I have been floating all weekend. Even work was fun tonight. There was a time when I would cry for no apparent reason, just break into tears at a sound or scent. Now I smile almost constantly. I am no longer just putting one foot in front of the other but walking with a bounce in my step. I think that the veil of grief is finally beginning to lift.

I can't attribute this all to you. Part of it is just the passing of time. Other people have helped immensely. I have struggled, fought back, and managed to keep most of my sanity (at least I think I have). And for all of that, I am a better person. I understand pain, loss, and compassion. I am better tuned into what is important in life and what I want out of mine. I am happy with who I am, more so than I have ever been before. It's just that it has been a long time since someone else was interested in who I am and that I was willing to share it with them.

So, in the chill of the early morning, I felt the warmth of your body against mine though you were miles away. And that warmth spread throughout my being. The simple touch of another human reminds me that I am alive. What should seem like the obvious, needed some reminding. And that is why I am indebted to you. I'm not sure that you understand that you can understand, but that's ok. This thank you is more for my benefit than it is for yours.

May you live in love for all of your days and may some of that love be mine.

Mark

As he hit print on the computer screen, he wiped away the tear that had been forming at the corner of his eye. This was not the time for that; there might not be another time for that. He folded the sheet of paper and slid it into the envelope that he borrowed from the department. As he headed out to check the town one last time before his shift ended, he stopped at the Post Office. He put a quarter and a dime in the machine and took his stamps. He wondered what her lips tasted like as he licked the larger of the two stamps and affixed it to the envelope he had addressed by hand.

"A15, Dispatch, report of a loose cow near the Main Street onramp," squawked from his lapel mike. He slid the letter into the slot and turned to leave. Bonnie Duncan's cow was apparently on the loose again. He was still smiling as he sat and drove north to deal with the bovine calamity.

Chapter Eight

College Town

November 13, 1996, 0805 Hours

He settled into his chair at the dining room table. He was tired. It had been a long graveyard shift. And it had not been without some excitement. He ran the day through his mind.

It had started when the new kid had spotted a car he didn't recognize at one of the drug houses in town. There had been two people in the car. The kid had stopped and talked with them. The man left and went into the house, but the girl stayed and talked with the kid. He was good looking and had a way about him. One of the dispatchers called him "Precious Angel Face." The kid used it to his benefit and got the woman to admit that Ron Knowles had been in the car with them, and that Knowles had gone into the house before he got there. Knowles was a thief and a methamphetamine addict with several felony warrants. The main entrance to the house was through the backyard, so the kid went there and demanded that Knowles came outside. The woman, perhaps realizing that she may have said too much, ran into the house when the kid checked the garage. The kid had heard her bar the door. Mark had arrived at about this time and after being briefed by the kid and took up a position at the front of the house. If Knowles was truly in the house, he was trapped now. The standoff stretched on for about thirty minutes until a sergeant arrived. As Knowles was on probation, had a search clause, and as this was his primary residence, they had elected to force entry. If Knowles wasn't inside, the kid would have some explaining to do.

The sergeant and the kid went to the back door while Mark had stayed at the front. They had broken down the rear door before and the sergeant knew that there was a 2X4 that held the door closed. But the window next to the door was wide open and the sergeant just reached in and began to slide the 2X4 out of the slots that held it in place. As he did so, the couple emerged from the bathroom naked. They had decided that while the police were demanding entry into their friend's house was a good time to take a shower. The man let the sergeant and the kid into the house. The kid wrapped them both in towels and stood guard while the sergeant quickly checked the house and then went to the front door where he let Mark in. Together he and the sergeant did a more thorough search of the residence. Knowles was not to be found. But there were wet footprints that went from the bathroom door to the area in the hallway beneath the attic access, and then back to the bathroom. In one of the bedrooms right off of the hallway was a ladder that looked out of place. The sergeant grabbed the ladder and set it up underneath the access. He tried to lift the plywood access cover out of the opening, but it would not budge. He went to his car and returned with a crowbar. As he started to pry the cover open, it came down in a spray of loose insulation and hit the sergeant in the head. Mark had seen a foot come through the opening. Knowles was in the attic.

They could hear him moving around above them, but he refused to come down. Then there was a crashing sound in one of the bedrooms. The sheetrock ceiling collapsed, and Knowles' rear end was visible through a hole. The sergeant tried to grab the seat of Knowles' pants, but wasn't quite fast enough. Instead, he was coated in loose insulation from head to foot. Knowles retreated away from the hole. And then, perhaps thinking that no one was watching the living room, he kicked another hole in the ceiling there. But the cascade of insulation was easily visible and when he tried to lower himself through the hole, Mark had been there to grab his leg. Knowles tried to retreat, but it was too late. He claimed that a nail was embedded in his thigh, but Mark had still kept the pressure on his leg. It was only when the kid climbed into the attic and threatened to pepper spray Knowles that he agreed to surrender. He dropped through the hole. Mark helped slow his descent, and then grabbed a wrist and began to apply pressure. He didn't want Knowles to think that he might be able to make a break for the door. The sergeant arrived within seconds and Knowles was cuffed and then searched. It hadn't been a nail embedded in his thigh, but a syringe that had been in his pocket. Mark had been sure he was making it up to try and get him to let go and delay his arrest by a few more minutes. Sometimes it sucked to be a bad guy.

The sergeant had gone home to clean up and put on a fresh uniform. The kid, beaming from ear to ear, had driven his hard-won arrest to the jail by way of the hospital. And Mark and returned to the station to write the report. He wasn't exactly sure how he had ended up with this detail, but that was alright with him. He kind of liked to write, but his sojourn in front of the computer had been short lived.

Dispatch had contacted him and sent him to a house that he had not visited before. He had been informed that a teen-age girl had entered into her ex-boyfriend's house and was threatening him with a knife. When Mark had gotten there, the two were wrestling on the floor. He grabbed the girl and held her against a wall. She began to sob, and all the fight went out of her. In talking to the participants, Mark had learned that the teenage couple had broken up. The young woman had taken it hard. She had armed herself with a steak knife and gone to her sweetheart's house. Her intentions were not exactly clear as her statements were conflicted. She may have had thoughts about slashing her wrists in front of her former lover. This would have been quite difficult, not to mention painful, with a steak knife. But when she arrived, she found a strange car in the driveway. Depression flashed into anger and she forced her way into the house. She was strong, and her ex was not a large young man. She headed for his bedroom to see who was there. When the ex-boyfriend saw the knife, he tried to stop her. A fight had ensued over the knife. Now she claimed that she just wanted to go home. Instead, he had driven her to juvenile hall and a small room with locked doors where she could contemplate what had been. The young man had a few cuts and scratches but had not been seriously hurt, and his new girlfriend was appropriately embarrassed.

So now, he was down two in-custody reports. He had sat back down in front of the keyboard. The rest of the night had cooperated, and he finished both reports just as his shift was ending. He had watched the sky lighten on his drive home, but the sun was hidden behind a wall of dark and foreboding clouds. It had started to drizzle as he had pulled into his driveway and the wind was picking up. The weather forecast was for an "atmospheric river" to form over the Pacific Ocean as several storm fronts piled up, one after another. It was going to rain. It would be a warm rain though, with the clouds coming from the southwest rather than from the Gulf of Alaska. That was alright with him, he liked rain.

Peacekeepers

As he sat and sipped a Diet Coke, his mind wandered from work to the girl. This happened several times a day. He pictured her smile, the way her cheeks widened and her eyes gleamed. He could look into those eyes for hours. His visions of her still made him smile and occasionally the warmth returned to his core, but he reminded himself that he barely knew this young woman and that he was in a pretty vulnerable place right now. This was not the right time to fall hard for someone. Logic and emotion don't belong in the same sentence.

It had been almost two weeks since he had seen her last. There had been no response to his letter. He was a bit surprised, as he thought it was a good letter. He had called a couple of times, but there was no answer. He told himself that he needed to be patient, that she had told him that it might be a while before he heard from her again. He didn't want to come across as desperate, but he did want to see her again. And as he thought about it, he admitted that he wanted to feel the euphoria that she brought forth. His mind likened it to a drug. He knew addicts that would do almost anything (and some who would do anything) for their next fix. He wondered what he had gotten himself into.

As he contemplated his fate, he took a look through the mail. One of his roommates had gathered it and left it on the table. It was mostly bills and advertisements, but as he got to the bottom of the pile, he found a post card. The picture was of a long sandy beach, but what caught his attention was the dark-complected young woman wearing a very skimpy bathing suit that occupied the foreground. The words "Greetings from Mexico" were emblazoned across the photo. He figured it had been sent to one of his roommates by a friend as a practical joke, but when he turned it over, he realized that it was addressed to him. And he recognized the handwriting. His heart began to beat faster as he read the few words written there:

Sorry that I have been out of touch for so long, but I had a chance to go to Baja with some friends and I took it. I just got home today and read your letter. Is there any chance you can come to my cabin on Friday night? I have something I want to try.

PK

He felt all warm and gooey inside. He was scheduled to work Friday night, but he would find someone to trade shifts with. As his smile crested into a huge grin, he pictured her once again in his mind. His eyes closed with the mental effort. He awoke with a start as his head fell towards the tabletop. It was time to stop daydreaming and think about getting some sleep. But when he laid down after a quick shower, he could still feel the smile that had spread from ear to ear. He wondered if he would dream of her. He hoped so. Gunner curled up next to him and made himself comfortable. And as the rain started to blow against his window, he drifted off.

Chapter Nine

College Town

November 15, 1996, 2145 Hours

It was Friday. His windshield wipers were beating a furious tempo as he drove into the hills and headed towards her cabin. He played the phone call back in his mind. PK had asked him to bring a towel, trunks if he wanted, and some warm clothes to change into. He had asked if they were going to go swimming. He liked swimming in the rain, but had no idea where they would go as it was the middle of November and all of the open water would be freezing. She hadn't answered with words, just kind of a little girl giggle. He hadn't seen that side of her before. Hot tubbing? He wondered if there was a hot tub at the main house, but he hadn't seen one, so, now he didn't know what to expect. But that was ok. He could feel the adrenaline flow through his body. He was excited about the evening. He was alive.

He passed the turnout with the view below her cabin. Tonight there was little to see, only the inside of clouds. He pulled into the driveway of the main house this time instead of parking on the street. Her pickup was there. He got out of his car and headed around the garage. As he rounded the corner, he saw the cabin, but there was only what looked like candlelight coming from the windows. As he got closer, he could hear reggae music over the sound of the wind and rain. He knocked on the door and she opened it after a short wait. Bob Marley was singing *One Love* inside.

Her hair was loose around her shoulders, but she had taken off her earrings. She still wore her pendant, however, as it was visible between the folds of a white bathrobe. The interior of the cabin was lit by a single candle near the back door. She bade him to enter and apologized for not meeting him at the door, but she had been busy in back and not heard his car over the wind. Her face was in shadow and he placed his hands on her shoulders, moving her closer to the candle. She didn't resist but walked backwards with him to the rear door. There he turned her so that the candlelight fell across one side of her face. He looked into her eyes. Light and shadow danced across her face and hair. This vision fascinated him. He could not remember eyes that had captivated him like this before. She returned his stare, looking squarely into his eyes. They held this position for what he thought was minutes, before she stirred.

"Come on, we don't have much time," she told him, then took off her bathrobe, hung it on a hook by the door and went outside.

He hadn't known what to expect, but the vision of her body, clad only in what appeared to be red bikini bottoms, had caused his jaw to drop. He quickly disrobed in the cabin. He thought about the shorts he had brought, but with an almost silent "fuck it," decided to leave them in the daypack he had brought. He headed for the door. Was there a hot tub in the woods?

Peacekeepers

The vision before him was wild. The wind rushed through the trees and their branches swayed in a wild dance. Rain was pouring down, driven at an angle by the southerly wind, and the girl was silhouetted in front of the fire. She had squatted down pushing the coals inward. The fire was partially shielded from the rain by a round, metal roof. The fire was mostly coals now and sizzled regularly as the wind blew in larger rain drops. He realized that she was moving the coals away from the wind driven rain. He watched from the shelter of the doorway, still not sure what to expect.

She stood and the silhouette formed a feminine figurine. He realized that there was a fair amount of blood flowing towards his groin and his excitement was going to be obvious if it was not already. And then she turned towards him. He tried to memorialize the image of her body in that flash of time when her breasts had been perfectly silhouetted by the fire. He was not sure he had ever seen anything quite so erotic. But now, she was in shadow and he was the one who was on display. Her head bobbed slightly as she took in the view and then he saw her signal him to come closer. He moved closer to her. The rain hit him. He had so much adrenalin running through him though that it felt more like a cool shower than a November rainstorm. He joined her and they moved to the far side of the fire where the coals were closer. She wrapped her arms around his waist and pulled him close. Once again, their eyes met. He could feel the warmth of her body against his, the softness of her breasts against his chest, his erect penis against her lower abdomen. She lifted her right leg and wrapped it around his upper thighs pulling him in even closer. If this was headed where he thought it was heading, he wondered why she had worn the bikini. He had never made love in the pouring rain before, had never even considered the idea. But there was a first time for everything.

But his train of thought was interrupted when she laid her head against his chest and began to sing softly.

Here comes the rain again
Falling on my head like a memory
Falling on my head like a new emotion
I want to walk in the open wind
I want to talk like lovers do
I want to dive into your ocean
Is it raining with you

He was completely taken aback; he didn't know what to say or do, so he just continued to hold her tight and share his warmth. For no matter how much adrenaline was coursing through his veins, he was getting cold, and he could tell that she was too. He guessed it was in the low 50s with the fire only providing a hint of warmth. Were the goose bumps on their arms the result of excitement, the cold, or maybe both?

But then she raised her eyes to his and stated, "So talk to me like lovers do."

He didn't know where to begin. So, he simply uttered the first thing that popped into his mind. "You're not like anyone else I have met before. You have a sensuosity that excites, a warmth that fills me with hope, but you are such a mystery. I can't read you at all. You constantly take me by surprise."

Her smile widened as she responded, simply, "My butt's getting cold." She then twisted in his arms so that they faced the same direction. He wrapped his arms around her belly, which was cold to the touch. She brought her arms up under his and pushed them upward so that his forearms lightly touched the bottom of her breasts.

"Let me explain a few things about myself then," she responded. "I was raised in SoCo, and there is a different culture there. It is based on a sense of self-sufficiency, a bit of hippie roots, and a disdain for the norm, or for authority. I believe in doing what feels good. When it no longer feels good, I stop. I am not the answer to your quest to find a companion. I cannot provide the permanency or exclusiveness you will seek."

He started to deflate as he heard these words, the November cold starting to seep into his core. But before his mood altered too much, she continued, "But right now, this feels good." And as she continued to speak, she swished her ass back and forth against his groin, "And I can tell that you think it feels good too. But you are going to have to wait to dive into my ocean."

"I don't understand what you mean," was his rather weak response. But he really did enjoy the feel of her rear end against his dick.

"You know, for an old guy, you're pretty naïve sometimes." She made a circle with the thumb and index finger of her left hand and showed it to him. "Ocean," she explained. Then she straightened the index finger of her right hand and inserted it into the circle of her left. "Diving." He couldn't see her face, but he was sure that she had a huge grin, while his jaw was somewhere in proximity to his navel.

"Oh, I get it. I have never heard of it being referred to as an ocean," was his timid response with just a hint of emphasis on 'it.'.

"It is salty and sweet, a cove where the mermaids play. Its waters ebb and flow in cycles like the tides. But for all the joy and beauty that is there, it is not without some risk, as you may yet find out. But now, tell me what it is like to lose a lover, as I am still trying to figure you out." And with those words, she spun around again so that she once again faced him.

His still erect penis was caught at an awkward angle, so he reached down and moved it so that it lay against her bare belly. Her smile widened and he tried to memorialize this vision once again. Rivulets were flowing down her face, around her eyes. They continued down her cheeks, over her neck, across her chest, and then diverged around the mounds of her breasts. Her eyes were dark in the limited light, but the smile was filled with warmth and affection. Her hair was soaked and stuck to her skin. He gently used his hands and moved it out of her face, so that it lay against her back. The goose bumps had spread to her chest and she had started to shiver. But she showed no sign that she intended to retreat to the cabin anytime soon. The firelight continued to dance across her skin but provided little warmth through the rain.

"Grief sucks," was his short answer to her question. But then he continued, "My sister once told me of a Mexican woman who gave her this explanation for what grief feels like. I think it describes it well and I have repeated it often. Depression is part of grief, maybe the biggest part. It is joined by denial, anger, and guilt. They all come and go, but depression is the most prevalent and the longest lasting. Grief is like being at the bottom of a deep pit. At the top, you can see the light of day, but there is no way to get out of the pit and you watch life pass you by as you sit alone in the darkness. You can hear laughter; you can hear joy. But you can't join in. It's just you and the darkness, but people walk by your pit. Some are friends, some are family, and both are trying to help. And some are the random encounters that are life. These people don't really know how to act around you, but they try. It's like they are throwing rocks into your pit. Some of the rocks hit you and hurt, but most just land in a pile. The rocks vary in size from pebbles to boulders. Time goes by. The pile of rocks gets bigger. Your exterior gets tougher, the rocks that hit don't hurt as much. And then one day, the pile is so big that you can climb up and escape from your pit. You don't remember everyone who threw a rock into your pit, but you remember the first, the ones that really hurt, and you most certainly remember the last one that allowed you to scramble to freedom."

To that, his smile deepened, and he kissed her gently on the forehead. "And that's why," he added. "I will always remember you. I don't think you will ever understand unless you, too, lose a lover."

She took his face in her hands. They were cold. But when she guided his lips to hers, there was nothing but warmth. Her tongue easily slipped between his teeth and he met the tip with his. They kissed, long and hard. When they pulled back to catch their breath, he kissed her gently again, this time on her lips. "Thank you for bringing me back to life," flowed from his lips as he kissed her one more time.

"I want to kiss like lovers do," she sang softly. They stood there, bodies pressed together for warmth, eyes locked on the others. And the rain poured down upon them both, and the wind blew through the trees. He wondered if he had ever felt anything more beautiful.

But she pulled away and started for the cabin door. "I have to leave, I have other commitments," was her simple explanation as she entered the cabin. His head dropped. Just when he thought he knew where he stood, she was gone again. He followed her to the cabin door, distraught that the evening appeared to be coming to an end, but realizing too, that he was thoroughly cold and needed to find shelter. He had never stood naked in a rainstorm, was not sure that he would do it again, but he wouldn't have missed it for the world.

When he got to the door, he saw that she had moved his daypack to the rug just inside. He grabbed his towel and dried off before entering.

He saw her bikini bottom lying on the floor in a small puddle. He picked it up, turned so that he was facing outside and gently rung most of the water out of it. He then hung it up on one of the hooks by the door. He didn't know what else to do with it. He then returned his focus to the interior of the cabin. The girl was by the woodstove. She had slipped into her bathrobe but held it open so that the warmth of the stove did not have to detour to find her skin. He continued drying off on the rug until he was confident that he would not drip on her floor. He crossed the room and stood behind her, his hands on her shoulders. His penis, which had grown limp from the cold, started to stir again.

"You must think I am a tease?" she asked without looking at him.

"Yeah, kind of," was his honest answer.

"I'm sorry. After you told me about what that song means to you, I wanted to make this a special night. But I don't have time to make the destination worthy of the journey, not tonight anyway. So, I am sorry, dear, but you are going to have to wait." And with that, she turned around in his arms once again, kissed him on the lips, and then deftly left him holding her robe.

He watched her naked body as she glided to the shower. There was a graceful beauty about the way her buttocks flowed into her thighs, the way her breasts rode high on her chest, her nipples hard and erect. He realized that in all the words that had been spoken on this night, he had never been more correct than when he said that he would never forget this woman. And then he turned to expose his buttocks to the warmth from the stove. He heard the water come on and the shower door open. He thought about trying to join her, but the shower stall was clearly designed just for one. So instead, he found the sweats he had packed into his bag and got dressed. He was still chilled, and while the night had not been what he had expected, nor was he ready for it to end, it had still been one of the most erotic of his life.

With that thought, he heard the water turn off, which caused him to look once more towards the shower. Steam clouded that corner, but he could make out her form as she exited the stall. Once again, water ran down her face, between her breasts and across her belly. He watched as the main rivulet slowed and was dispersed by her patch of coarse, blonde pubic hair. He wondered if his gaze was inappropriate. But when he raised his glance once more to her face, he saw a different emotion. Her face was sad, almost remorseful.

"I'm sorry, I almost changed my mind and asked you to stay. I'm not done with you yet, please don't go away mad. But I have a family commitment tonight in Weedtown that I can't ignore. My family is the center of my universe and I have to be there. I was afraid that the weather would change, and I would not have the opportunity to stand in the rain with you for a long time. It was something I wanted to do, something I wanted to share with you, but I didn't want to hurt you or leave you hanging, so to speak. I didn't think it through completely."

"I'm not mad, disappointed a bit, but not mad. Tonight was one of the best nights of my life," was the simple and honest answer he gave. "I wouldn't have missed it for anything. You have nothing to apologize for." He closed the ground between them and gave her a gentle hug and a kiss. He could feel the dampness of her skin through his sweatshirt. He couldn't tell if the water flowing around her eyes was from the shower or tears. He kissed her gently on her cheeks and could detect just a hint of salt.

"There's no need for tears," he whispered in her ear. He then took a towel and handed it to her and found another in small dresser. "Work on drying your hair and I'll dry the rest." He carefully ran the towel across her back, between her cheeks and down each leg. She shimmied just a bit with his actions but didn't object. When he reached her feet, she turned. He repeated the actions, drying her shoulders, chest, breasts and belly. As the towel descended between her thighs, he kissed her belly. When he was done, he stood again and faced her, his excitement evident by the bulge in his sweatpants.

She smiled at him, the sadness gone. "You're kind of a tease yourself," she stated before taking the towel from him. She turned around and dried those areas that he had not done an adequate job on, beneath her breasts and between her legs. This was the only sign of modesty she had displayed so far. She then went to her dresser and put on panties and a bra. She stood in front of her mirror and reached for her brush.

"I know you're in a hurry, but can I ask a favor? Can I brush your hair?" he asked.

She looked at him in the mirror and then handed him the brush. "Just go slow and be gentle. It's kind of tangled."

He took the brush and stood behind her, gathering her hair with one hand and moving the brush through it with the other. He took his time, working through the tangles. She was patient. He concentrated on her hair, not seeing the look on her face in the mirror. His mind was concentrating on the feel of hair sliding through his fingers, the scent of her body, earthy with just a hint of musky sex. He didn't realize the effect this was having on the rest of his body until she leaned back against him. Then he realized that he was hard again.

"You gotta go," was what he heard in a low voice. But when he looked in the mirror and saw her face, she was smiling. Then she ground her rear end into his groin making it evident that she knew he was aroused. "You gotta go, or my family will disown me forever."

"Can I ask a question before I go?" he whispered. "You're obviously not bashful. Why did you wear the bikini?"

"I knew that we would be close in the rain. Parts just tend to line up. I wanted a barrier to make sure that we didn't reach our destination prematurely. So, I decided that one of us needed to wear pants. I hope that you didn't mind."

He turned her around, looked into her eyes one more time and kissed her passionately. She joined his kiss, and then gently placed both of her hands on his chest and pushed him away. "Go, just go," she whispered. "Please, before I make you stay."

He gathered his clothes and found his raincoat. He looked at her as she stood watching him. She hadn't moved. He watched as her chest rose and fell with each breath. He tried to read her body language. Did she really want him to leave? He honestly didn't want to, but he would do whatever this woman asked him to. He looked for a sign, didn't see one and opened the door. He didn't see her turn back towards the mirror or the tears that formed at the corners of her eyes.

Chapter Ten

Small Town

November 17, 1996, 0349 Hours

It was almost 4:00 in the morning. Mark was sitting in his patrol car, tucked into King Street where he could watch the last house on 4th Street before it ran into Queen. He had been sitting here for the last forty minutes. There was a pickup truck in the driveway that he had not seen before. He had not seen it arrive, but he was hoping that he would see it leave.

His feet were still cold. He had not realized how cold he was until he got into his car and started down the hill. Adrenaline and lust were wonderful drugs. He had cranked up the heater as high as it would go, but the chill had remained. Even his own long, hot shower had not fully returned warmth to his body, although it had provided a release for the sexual tension that had built up over the course of the evening. He went to bed with cold feet and when he woke up, despite Gunner's best efforts, they were still chilled. Now he sat in his patrol car. He had turned off the engine, and consequently the heater, in an effort to remain undetected. There was no wind or rain this morning to mask the noise of the car and sounds carried in the morning quiet.

For most of the time that he had been doing surveillance, he had been dissecting the previous night at PK's cabin. She was unpredictable, that was for sure. But she was also up front, sort of anyway, and had explained that she could not or would not provide what he was looking for. But as he thought about this, he decided that was ok. He had been kind of a hippie when he was a kid, trying to follow in his older siblings' footsteps. It had not lasted, but there were pictures of him with hair down to his collar somewhere. Perhaps he could handle a little hedonistic behavior of his own. *As long as it feels good*, he thought to himself with a smile.

And as the smile formed on his lips, he saw the back-porch light come on. A man exited the door and headed towards the pickup. He waited until he heard the truck start before turning the key and starting his patrol car. The truck's headlights came on, but he waited. The pickup backed out of the driveway and turned towards him. He watched as the truck turned from 4th Street to Queen and started to cross over the freeway. He put the car in gear and started to follow, only turning on the lights as he came to the stop sign at the intersection with Queen. He accelerated rapidly, not wanting to lose sight of the pickup. He lost it just briefly, but as he crested the overpass, he saw the truck taking the northbound onramp to the freeway. He followed. Hopefully, the driver of the pickup would just think he was another car on the road.

They both merged onto the freeway and headed north. He started to look for probable cause to stop the truck. He wanted to find out who this late-night visitor was if nothing else. The pickup's lights all worked; the license plate had a current sticker. He watched his speedometer. The truck might be speeding. He settled in behind the truck and started to pace it. His speedometer read 68 miles per hour. It was only three miles an hour over the limit, but it was a violation. *Best I can do*, he thought to himself. He turned on the red light. The truck slowed but didn't pull over. He flipped the switch another notch and the rotating lights came on.

"Dispatch, A15, traffic," he spoke as he keyed the microphone.

She responded with "A15 is traffic."

"A15 is traffic, northbound Big Highway approaching Main, on 1Lincoln24896." He was proud that his vision was still good enough that he could read the license plate.

The dispatcher parroted his words, "Roger, A15 is traffic on 1Lincoln24896, northbound Big Highway approaching main." He realized that he was probably pulling her away from a late-night TV show and she was probably calling him something that was slightly offensive. But that was part of the relationship with dispatchers. You relied on them for information as well as the safety they could provide and in return, they got to call you names when you did something stupid or that caused them some slight discomfort.

"Dispatch, A15 is still rolling, passing Main." The truck had not stopped but continued to drive northbound at about 40 miles per hour.

"Roger, A15, still rolling passing Main," she parroted. They used this system of repeating information to make sure that it was correct. "A15, speed, traffic level and reason for stop?" she asked.

"Dispatch, A15, speed is 40, negative to light traffic, stop is for speed, negative pursuit at this time," he answered. The dispatcher was getting a bit ahead of herself. She would need this information if a pursuit was declared as she would need to wake up his supervisor and advise her of the pursuit and traffic conditions. The supervisor would then likely have him discontinue as the risk wasn't worth the known gain. So, unless and until the driver goosed the throttle and took off like a bat out of hell, this was just a traffic stop that was taking a little longer than normal for the driver to find a safe place to pull over. And it was the unknown that he was interested in. Who was this guy and what was he doing in Small Town?

"Dispatch, A15 still rolling, approaching the bridge over Big River," he told the dispatcher.

"Roger, A15, still rolling. Q32 is enroute from River City to back." He thought that as they got to the bridge, the driver would either make a run for it or decide to finally pull over. But they crossed the bridge, still going way below the speed limit until they got to the far side of the bridge and continued for another 200 yards. Then the truck slowed, signaled a right turn, and finally came to a stop on the shoulder.

"Dispatch, A15, final stop is just south of the mill entrance."

"Roger, A15, final stop at mill entrance," she parroted again. She then added, "1Lincoln24896 is clear and current on an 86 Toyota registered to Sunshine Garvey out of Weedtown."

"A15 copies," he responded. Weedtown most likely meant marijuana, but he had never heard of Tammy Wright selling marijuana. Who was this guy and what was he doing at her house? And Sunshine did not sound like a Hispanic name, more like his parents were hippies; that suggested the weed scene too.

The truck rolled to a stop and he parked about thirty feet behind it. He left on the rotating lights in the light-bar mounted on the top of his patrol car. Red and blue flashes lit up the landscape around him. He also flipped on his takedown lights; bright, white lights that were mounted in the same light-bar. They lit up the truck like it was daytime, and in theory, blinded the driver to his approach. In the distance, he could see another set of rotating lights headed his direction. There wasn't much to do at this time in the morning, and it was a chance to drive fast and see what was going on in the town next door without having to take paper. He wouldn't mind the company. And if this turned out to be something interesting, it would be much safer.

He walked around the back of his car and approached the truck on the passenger side. This kept him out of the travelled lanes of the freeway and was considered safer. As he got to the truck he used his flashlight to illuminate the areas of the truck bed that were in shadow. The bed was empty. He did the same thing with the cab as he got closer. The driver had seen his silhouette as he approached and had rolled down the passenger side window. As he looked in the window, he saw that there was trash on the floorboards, mostly junk food wrappers and beverage containers. There was a closed cardboard box, taped shut, on the passenger seat. The glove compartment was open and only contained paperwork. He didn't see any weapons in the cab. There was a very faint odor of burned marijuana coming from the interior. The driver had his hands on the steering wheel. *He's been in this position before*, Mark thought to himself.

"May I see your license, registration, and proof of insurance?" he asked the driver. The driver had already gathered the required documents and handed them to him.

As he prepared to turn and return to his car, the man asked him, "Officer, why did you pull me over? I wasn't doing anything wrong. I kept waiting for you to pass me, but you never did."

He glanced at the license in his hand and replied, "Mr. Garvey, I pulled you over for speeding. I clocked you at 68 miles per hour in a 65 zone."

The man tried to keep his cool, but still uttered, "You got to be fucking kidding me! It's 4:00 in the morning!"

He responded with, "Please stay in your truck and I'll be right back." He didn't want to stay and discuss the legitimacy of the stop with him. It wasn't about traffic safety at all.

When he got back to his car, he reached in and turned off the rotators. There had been an informational bulletin put out by the Highway Patrol recently that suggested that rotating lights were more likely to attract drunk drivers than those that just blinked. He retreated to the trunk lid of the car and examined the documents he had been provided. He was joined by Officer Cook who had pulled up behind his vehicle.

"What do you got?" Officer Cook asked.

"I saw this guy leaving one of our drug houses. I have a new informant who told me that a Hispanic guy drops off an ounce of meth there every Friday. I thought it might be him. But this guy is white, he's from Weedtown, and it looks more like a marijuana deal. I didn't think Tammy Wright dealt in marijuana, so now I am just a bit confused."

He keyed his mike, "Dispatch, A15, request 27, 29, and NCIC by number."

"Go ahead A15," came back over the radio.

"A15, 27, 29, and NCIC on Zebra8765678," he told her as he read Garvey's driver's license number off of the card.

There was a brief pause until the dispatcher came back on the radio, "A15, Garvey is valid, but is Code-6 I-Ida, NCIC is clear." Garvey had failed to show up in court on an infraction citation. He couldn't book him into the jail on this warrant, but he could arrest him and search him and his truck. If he didn't find anything, he would write him another citation with a new court date for the warrant. *Bingo*, he thought to himself.

"Dispatch, A15 copies. What's the warrant for?" he asked the dispatcher.

94

"A15, it looks like it's for riding a motorcycle without a helmet," she answered.

So, the guy's not real smart, he thought to himself. He returned to the truck, this time approaching the driver's side door after checking traffic to make sure it was safe. When he got to the door, he knocked on the widow to get the driver's attention. Garvey rolled down the window.

"Mr. Garvey, would you please get out of your truck," he requested.

"Ok, but what did I do?"

"You have a warrant for your arrest. It appears you failed to appear in traffic court for riding a motorcycle without a helmet. Would you please step out of the truck?" he told Garvey, adding a slightly more demanding tone to the last sentence.

"Bullshit," Garvey stated, "I took care of that warrant months ago."

"Mr. Garvey, would you please get out of the truck," he repeated. This time it was clearly a demand and not a question. As he said this, he noticed that Officer Cook had approached the passenger side of the pickup and was illuminating the interior of the cab. He saw that Garvey saw it too. He took one step backwards, just to make sure that he wasn't in a crossfire situation should Garvey try and use a weapon. Garvey seemed frozen, unable to make a decision to cooperate, fight or flee. Mark reached forward and opened the door of the pickup, the first step in dragging Garvey out of the pickup if it came to that.

"Mr. Garvey, is there anything I can do to convince you to get out of your truck before Officer Cook and I are forced to remove you?" he asked. It was a verbal judo line he had learned in training. He had never given the line much credibility, but he didn't really want to fight with the guy on the side of the freeway either. There wasn't much traffic, but it would only take one car to ruin everyone's day.

Garvey didn't move.

"A15, status check?" came over his radio.

"A15 is 10-6," was his reply.

"Roger, A15 is busy, negative Code-4."

Officer Cook had opened the passenger side door. If they had to wrestle with the guy, they would try and take him out that side to stay out of traffic. Officer Cook was still illuminating the inside of the cab with his flashlight. His light stopped moving and stayed on one spot. "Mark, there's a gun under the seat!" Officer Cook exclaimed loudly as he drew his weapon.

"Garvey, put your fucking hands on the window frame now," Cook demanded loudly. "There's nothing in this truck worth getting shot over."

He saw Garvey's eyes blink. He didn't know if it was the tone, the f-bomb he had used, or something else that snapped Garvey out of his inertia. Garvey slowly, palms open and fingers extended, showed him his hands and then placed them on the window frame as directed. Mark holstered his firearm, knowing that Cook still had Garvey covered. He reached out with both of his hands and took control of Garvey's left wrist, while telling him to leave his other hand where it was. Garvey complied. He placed Garvey's wrist into a twist lock. He then told him to swing his feet out of the cab and place them on the ground. Garvey again complied. Mark pushed the truck door open all the way with his foot so that he would have more room to work. He then applied just a little twisting torque to Garvey's wrist and brought it down and behind his back. Garvey didn't contest the movement and it caused him to move so that he was now standing and facing away from Mark. He took a pair of handcuffs from his belt with his right hand, while still twisting Garvey's wrist slightly with his left. He slipped the cuff around Garvey's wrist. Mark moved his left hand to control the cuffs and reached for Garvey's right hand with his own. He again applied twisting pressure to the wrist and moved it behind Garvey's back to the waiting cuff. Once Garvey was securely handcuffed, he adjusted them to make sure that they were snug, but not too tight, and then double locked them with his handcuff key so that they wouldn't get any tighter.

"Dispatch, A15 is Code-4 with one in custody," he spoke into his radio microphone.

"A15 is Code-4, one in custody."

Once he had Garvey securely handcuffed, he moved him to the passenger side of his patrol car. Mark got out another paper bag and donned a pair of latex gloves. He then began to search Garvey, starting at the collar of his coat. He didn't find anything, so he moved down, checking the coat pockets. In the first one, he found a sandwich-sized Ziplock bag. Inside the bag was a golf ball sized chunk of a dirty-white, powdery substance. The bag had a chemical smell. Mark was pretty sure that it was meth, but he had never seen such a large quantity.

He asked Garvey, "Is this what I think it is?"

"Fuck you," was his response. He then added, "Who set me up? Was it that fucker, Rickstraw? Is that why he asked me to do his deliveries tonight?"

Mark didn't answer, but filed away the name. He didn't know who that was, but it seemed like it might be worth finding out. He continued searching, and in the other coat pocket, he found another bag with another large chuck of dirty white powder. He placed both bags inside of the paper bag. Garvey was wearing a leather vest under the coat. He continued to remove Ziplock bags from Garvey's vest pockets. He wondered if the lunch bag was big enough. And then there was more in his pants pockets. When he was done he found five bags, each holding about an ounce of suspected methamphetamine and four smaller bags that looked more like an eighth of an ounce. Garvey's wallet only held about forty dollars, and it went into the bag too. He didn't find any weapons or drug paraphernalia, but he did find a list of addresses located throughout Big Tree County. Tammy Wright's house was on the list. Interestingly, so was Joe McDonald's. That, too, went in the bag. He placed Garvey in the back seat of his patrol car.

Meanwhile, Officer Cook was searching the cab of the truck. When Mark arrived, Cook showed him what he had found. He had the items laid out on the hood of the pickup. There was a loaded revolver, two speedloaders filled with ammunition, five sealed bags of marijuana bud weighing about a pound each in the cardboard box, and an envelope filled with cash. The bills were 100s and it looked to be a couple of thousand dollars. Quite the haul from a single traffic stop. He examined the revolver.

"Dispatch, A15, request a 29 on a firearm."

"A15, go ahead."

He keyed his mic again, "Serial number is 1245878. It's a Smith and Wesson Model 66, .357 revolver."

"Roger A15," came over the radio and there was a slight pause before the dispatcher responded to his request to determine if the firearm was stolen. "A15, the firearm is clear and registered to your subject out of Weedtown."

"A15 copies."

He asked Officer Cook, "Do you have a bag phone in your car?"

"Yeah, I have one, what are you thinking?"

"Do you think your department's guy on the Task Force would want to talk to this guy, at least enough to wake him up at 4:30 in the morning? We have five and a half ounces of meth, five pounds of weed, and a gun. He might think that is worth getting up early for."

"Won't know if we don't ask him," Officer Cook replied with a wicked grin. And with that, he headed back to his car to call the dispatcher.

The rest of the morning was a blur. They transported Garvey to the River City station after arranging to have his truck towed. There they met Agent Mulhouse from the Task Force. This was an organization run by the State's Bureau of Narcotic Enforcement. The larger departments in the County provided one and sometimes two officers to the Task Force. In exchange they received a share of the asset forfeiture that was taken in. They worked on all kinds of drug cases but seemed to spend more time on marijuana as that was where the money was in Big Tree County. Agent Mulhouse took their evidence and control of their prisoner. He would try and get him to cooperate in exchange for leniency on his charges. Sometimes it worked, sometimes it didn't, but like Officer Cook stated, you won't know if you don't try. He had returned to his station just before his shift was supposed to end. Because it was an in-custody case he had to have his report done before he went home and fell asleep. So he bought himself a fresh Diet Coke at the gas station and plopped his tired rear-end in front of the computer terminal. Luckily, it was pretty straight forward. He came, he saw, he had seized. The next step would be to see if he had enough probable cause for a search warrant for Tammy Wright's house. But that would have to wait until he got some sleep. And then he noticed that his feet weren't cold anymore as he started to type.

Chapter Eleven

Café on the Old Highway

November 17, 1996, 0349 Hours

The note had surprised him when it came. It had been more than a week since the rainy night at the cabin. He had called a couple of times, but there had been no answer. He almost drove by to see if she was there, but he thought that might be an invasion of her privacy. He had almost convinced himself that perhaps this was over. Confidence, when it came to women, was not his strong suit. But then the note came in the mail:

Mark,

I'm sorry dear, but I am still at my sister's house in SoCo and they don't have a phone or a computer. I want to explain a little bit about why I had to leave the other night, and a little more about me. I think I owe you that much. Can you meet me for breakfast at the café next to the high school on the Old Highway on Thursday? If I remember correctly, you have to work the night before.

Hugs and kisses

Peacekeeper

PS – Please don't dress like a cop.

He still wasn't sure what to expect as he drove the Old Highway. She hadn't specified a time or a way to contact her, so he had just driven south when he got off of work. He brought clothes and changed out of his uniform, and he wore a beanie to hide his closely cropped hair. The rain had returned, and a gentle mist was falling on his windshield as he drove through the stands of old growth forest that made this route one of the most beautiful roads in the world. The river was rising and flowed with gusto out his window. Maybe he should just enjoy the beauty in the world and let what was going to happen, happen without trying to analyze it first. After all, he was trying to return to his hippie roots. He smiled, then he pulled over into a turnout. He got out of his car and watched the river flow by. Tendrils of fog drifted through the treetops. The colors were muted in the overcast, early morning light and it almost looked like an Ansel Adams photo: black, white and a thousand shades of gray. Birdcalls sounded, and then were drowned out by a truck rumbling by on the nearby freeway. His mind calmed and another faint smile crossed his lips. *This smiling thing was getting out of control*, he thought as he climbed back into the car and headed the last few miles to the café.

The trees thinned as he entered the clump of businesses that surrounded the high school. This school serviced a huge area, and it was not unusual for the students to have to ride the bus for more than two hours each way to get there. It was still early and only a few students walked the streets. He saw PK's truck before he saw the café. He pulled into a perpendicular parking spot and parked. So as not to dress as a cop, he left his off-duty gun in the car, stuffed under the seat. He got out, stretched, and breathed in the late fall air. He loved this time of year. The air was cool and crisp. The hardwoods still had a few leaves attached and these provided some color to the forest backdrop. He walked up the steps and pulled open the café's front door.

She was sitting with her back to him in far corner of the restaurant, but she was easy to pick out. Her blond ponytail extended from her Bob Marley beanie, and she was wearing the same wool sweater that she wore at the beach. A raincoat was draped over the back of the chair. He moved to her table and drank in her smile as she saw him. He asked if he could join her, and still smiling, she bade him to sit. She wore the abalone earrings again, and although the pendant was hidden beneath her sweater, he could see the thong around her neck. He knew that she had more jewelry, but this appeared to be what she preferred. As he settled his bulk into a chair, he realized that his back was against the far wall of the dining room. And from this vantage point, he could see anyone who came in. It was the preferred seat for most police officers. They were professional people watchers. But it also made it more difficult for anyone else to recognize PK unless they knew her form well. He wondered if this was intentional on her part, or maybe it was just coincidence. Was anything with this woman coincidence? And then he looked into her eyes and all those thoughts evaporated. They sat, neither one speaking, like this until the waiter came and asked if he wanted coffee. He asked for a Diet Coke instead and the reverie was broken.

She spoke first, "Thanks for meeting me here, I know it is out of your way, but I don't have a lot of time and there aren't many breakfast places until River City."

"Thanks for inviting me," was his response. "I've missed you and I can't seem to stop thinking about that night in the rain."

"Let me explain a bit," she said. "When I first saw you at the protest, I could see the kindness in your eyes even though you were dressed like a storm trooper. I was curious. I asked a couple of people I know who live in Small Town. They told me that for a cop you were alright, a ringing endorsement if ever there was one. It probably wouldn't have amounted to anything except that you showed up at my restaurant. I decided to give you my number on a whim. I didn't know exactly what to expect, but I thought you would be like most men, all hands and a hard dick. And if you had been, it would have been one, done, and on with the rest of my life. I have never shagged a policeman and wondered if you would be any different, but instead, you seemed reserved, polite almost to a fault. You spoke well and your eyes drew me in. And so rather than just a bit of fun, I wanted to get to know you, to see what made you tick. I could see the pain inside of you, but I could also see you come alive when we were together. That made me feel good, much better than a quick jump in the sack. And so I found time to spend with you. But as you are learning, time is something I don't have in great abundance. You should take it as a compliment that I elect to spend as much with you as I do even though it may not amount to much."

The waiter came to take their order, but neither one of them had looked at the menu. They both glanced at the options quickly and made a hurried choice. He selected chorizo and eggs, while she asked for a veggie omelet. The waiter left with their order and she returned to her explanation.

"I probably shouldn't be telling you this, but I think you need to know what you have probably already assumed. My life has been split between College Town and SoCo. My parents split up when I was in grade school and, so I have bounced back and forth between the two. My mother spends most of her time in College Town, but still has property out by the coast. My father lives near my mother's property. He's in the weed business. My mother leases the majority of her property to a friend. He's in the same business. That is the main source of her income. This was the culture I was raised in. The police, with their helicopters, are the enemy. They come in the night with guns and terrify everyone they touch. You don't talk to them, you don't tell them anything. You don't call them, but rather you handle problems yourself. If you can't take care of it by yourself, the rest of the community will help out. Even the conversation we are having now is difficult for me. Like your grief, I don't think you can truly understand unless you were brought up in it. That is one of the main reasons that I cannot provide what you seek. My family, large parts of it anyway, and my culture would cast me out. So, I am torn between the affection I feel for you and the roots of my being.

"Last week, I had to leave because I needed to help my sister. She lives with our grandfather, her husband, and their two kids. Her man has made some bad choices lately and she had to make a business trip. Normally, if she were going to be gone, one or both of my parents would have helped with the kids and grandpa. But this trip was unplanned. My dad's at a music festival in San Diego and my mother is travelling with her sister, so, I was the only one that she could count on. They were in pretty desperate straits and the trip could not be postponed. She's on her way back now and they should have enough money to get by for now. So, even though I didn't want you to leave, I had my roots pulling me away. And I couldn't very well explain to my family that I had met a new man. I'm sorry that this is the way it is, but it is the way it is. I have to keep the details about you from my family and friends and vice versa."

105

He digested her words for a few moments before speaking. "I am honored that given my profession, you feel comfortable enough to share this with me. And you are correct; nothing that you have told me is a surprise, but it doesn't change a thing as far as I am concerned."

The waiter brought their food as he finished speaking. The chorizo was surprisingly good. They took turns eating while the other one spoke. In this way, he learned of her growing up in the hills near the coast. She attended a school that only had about five or six students per grade. The school had a small marijuana garden that was tended by the kids and the profit, if there was one, was used to fund field trips. She spoke of her own garden at her father's house that she used to fund her world travels as well as her education. She had already spent one summer in Europe and another in South America. But she had plans beyond marijuana. Her primary love in life was the beauty all around her. She wanted to make sure that it existed for her children and her children's children. She thought that the best way to do this was inside of the system, rather than as an agitator. Consequently, she had elected to study forestry and environmental engineering. She intended to try and get a job with one of the regulatory agencies and rise high enough that she could affect real change. She realized that she might be seen as deserting the cause by some of her compatriots, but she would accept that in exchange for being able to actually make a difference rather than just talk about it.

And in turn, he talked about growing up in Southern California, how he never realized what a good childhood he had until he met some kids that didn't have the advantages that he did. How he had always loved the sound of the wind in the trees and wanted to live where the sound was common and not just occasional. He had studied forestry in school to further that ambition. The more he learned, the more he had liked it.

He had chosen harvest systems as a subject of particular interest, admitting that part of it was the adrenaline it invoked. He had moved to Big Tree County with the thought of starting his own logging company with some money he had inherited. Instead, he learned quickly that would be a great way to lose what money he had. But he had enjoyed working in the woods as a logger. It allowed him to earn a decent wage, but to still have winters off to play. He talked about playing rugby for the university team even though he was never a student there. And he talked about his decision to change careers as the working seasons in the woods got shorter and shorter due to the new regulations being imposed on the industry. He admitted that he liked to shoot guns and drive fast, so he thought that law enforcement would be the perfect job for him. He again admitted that there was a part of him that liked the sudden surge of adrenaline that came with the job. That, and each day was different from the last with no two calls ever being really the same. But the job also had downsides. He often saw people on some of the worst days of their lives, sometimes the worst day. It was hard not to become jaded and cynical, but as long as he could avoid the attention of his supervisors, he had no intentions of leaving law enforcement.

Neither one of them spoke about romantic partners, past, present or future.

As the waiter cleared the table and brought the bill, Mark reached for it. But before he could grasp it, she took it from the table.

"Let me buy, please," she asked. "It was my invitation and I really do have the money."

He acquiesced and watched as she went to the cash register and removed a wallet from her purse. He left a ten-dollar bill on the table for a tip and joined her. When the tab had been paid, they both went outside to where their vehicles waited.

She looked at a watch she wore on her wrist. "I have a few minutes left; follow me and park where I turn off of the highway."

"Ok," he responded. He was happy to have the morning continue.

They drove north together and dropped down the hill that led away from the business district. At the bottom of the hill, she turned left into a turnout that led to a dirt road that accessed the river. The gate was open. As directed, he parked his car in the turnout. When he got out, he saw that she had the passenger door of her truck open for him. He climbed in. The interior was worn, but clean. There was the odor of burnt marijuana in the air. As she put the truck into gear, she shifted into four-wheel-drive. The road was muddy and filled with large puddles. They splashed their way onto the gravel riverbar and she parked to the side to allow other vehicles to pass. There was another pickup with a small boat trailer parked near the water. The other truck appeared to be vacant. He glanced back towards the highway and realized that it was screened by the large trees. They were alone, at least for now. She got out and he followed.

"I don't really have much time," she told him, "but I wanted to spend just a few minutes in your arms and there were too many people in town that know my family. I hope you don't mind the short side trip."

She wrapped her arms around his neck and pulled him close. Again, their eyes locked. He held her around the waist. They swayed slowly together, the river providing the rhythm. No words were spoken, but their eyes conveyed the affection that they felt for each other. They stayed locked together for minutes, the mist forming drops on their hats, hair, and eyebrows. She finally broke the trance.

"I really do have to go," she whispered. "I have a friend filling in for me, but her shift at the hospital starts in two hours."

She kissed him gently on the lips and led him back to the pickup. He climbed in and rode in silence during the short drive back to his car. When she stopped he leaned across the cab and found her lips with his. This was not a short kiss, more of the kind where you have to come up for air, and he eventually did.

As he opened the door, he spoke softly, "Have I told you how beautiful you are, both inside and out?"

"Thank you for noticing," was her simple reply, the same one that she had used before. He smiled and she returned the unspoken declaration. And then she shifted back into two-wheel-drive, and with a wave, she was gone.

He got into his car and the radio came on as he started the engine. His normal station didn't reach this far into the hills, so he had switched to the oldies station that could be heard all over the county. As he pulled onto the highway, The Turtles finished *So Happy Together.* This song made him think of Karen, for there was a time when he wanted it to be their first dance song at their wedding. But he realized that his memories of her were starting to fade; no longer was her face in sharp focus. He wondered if she could see him now, and if she would be happy for him. He couldn't answer that. Then the commercial break ended, and Roberta Flack began to sing *The First Time Ever I Saw Your Face."* He hadn't heard this song in a long time. He turned up the volume and listened to Flack's soft and sultry voice. By the end of the second verse, all thoughts of Karen were long gone, replaced by more current visions. And then came the third verse:

And the first time ever I lay with you
I felt your heartbeat so close to mine
And I knew our joy would fill the earth
And last till the end of time my love

All he could envision was the girl in his arms amid the pouring rain. She accompanied him all the way home and was still with him when he crawled between the sheets. Gunner forgave him for his lack of attention and curled up beside him as Mark started to snore.

Chapter Twelve

Small Town

December 16, 1996, 0745 Hours

Mark was having a hard time keeping his eyes open. It was 7:45 and he had been told to wait for the chief to show up this morning. He wasn't sure what this was about, but he couldn't think of anything he had done to get into trouble, at least the kind of trouble that required a visit to the chief's office. So, he sat and tried to keep his eyes open.

It had been a pretty quiet night except for two horses that had gotten loose. He had found them grazing in the park. They had not protested when he looped dog leashes around their necks and tied them off to a fence. They had just continued to eat the lush grass on the edge of the softball field. As he prepared to take off to find their owner, a truck had backfired on the freeway and both horses bolted. The leashes drew tight and started to choke the animals. Their fear increased and they pulled even harder. The chain link fence started to lose its shape, but the leashes did not break. In their flailing, both horses had fallen to the ground. He had quickly stopped the car and ran to the animals, drawing his folding knife as he went. The nylon, drawn taunt from the horses' struggles, parted quickly under his blade. He quickly removed the remains of his leashes from the horses' necks. They stood and began to graze again, apparently unfazed. But they wouldn't let him get quite as close as before. He had left them to eat and again went in search of an owner. He had found her about a half hour later and gotten her out of bed. She was apologetic as she walked the animals back to a half-assed corral she had erected with electric wire on a vacant lot next to her house. He was just glad that the animals had not been hit by a car. He had seen the remains of a cow that had been hit by four cars on the freeway. None of the cars had been drivable afterwards and there had been bovine entrails covering over 100 yards of freeway. He had washed his car afterwards, but even so all the dogs in town had taken an increased interest in his car for days.

As he recalled the pure fear in the horses' eyes as he tried to free them, his own eyes closed. And the vision changed. He and PK had met twice more since their breakfast together. Both times it had been on a riverbar, both times it had been raining lightly. He recalled the beads of moisture in her hair. They had stood together in nature's beauty, listening to music of the river. But he couldn't recall a single thing other than the beauty that he had held in his arms. He had lost all other focus, captivated by those dark blue irises that said so much with no words. His other senses had also been fixated on the girl, the silkiness of her skin under his fingertips, the scents of musk and earth in his nose, and the hint of saltiness when he had nibbled on her ear. These remembrances filled his head as it slowly lowered to the tabletop in front of him.

"Coltrane, wake up!" roaring in his ear was the next thing his brain consciously processed. But even this wasn't enough to remove the warm glow from his belly. He followed his chief into his office.

"Have a seat, Coltrane," the chief requested. While he made himself comfortable, the chief continued. "I got a call from the Task Force yesterday. They have a search warrant for Sunshine Garvey's property in SoCo and they want you to participate. They think they may find evidence of drug operations in Small Town and they would rather you followed up on any leads here while they look at the bigger picture."

The chief continued: "You need to be at the CalFire Station outside of Weedtown at 0600 for briefing. Take a patrol car, but don't get it stuck on some back road in the middle of nowhere. It will be a burned hulk before we can get it out. You'll probably have to ride into the site in someone else's rig. Let's see, what else do I have for you. I've arranged to have Bill cover your shift tonight so that you can get some sleep. Be more awake tomorrow morning than you were this morning. Don't do anything I wouldn't do. Now go home and get some sleep and leave that poor girl alone for a couple of days." There was a slight pause and then the chief added, "That was good work out there on the freeway the other morning."

He got up and stumbled out of the office. He was almost as surprised that the chief knew about PK as he was that the Task Force had asked him to go on the warrant. The new chief was better than the old one, but only time would tell if he could be trusted. And he wondered about the compliment as he was leaving. He couldn't recall a single time that the old chief had praised his work, at least not to his face.

He was too tired to be excited about the warrant, much less the new chief, as he stripped off his gear. Instead, visions of the girl reentered his mind. He moved like a zombie as he climbed into his car. Fortunately, the traffic was light, and although he could not remember a single thing about the drive, he managed to get home safely. His mind had been filled with memories. And those memories became dreams as his mind relaxed upon contact with his pillow.

Chapter Thirteen

Weedtown

December 17, 1996, 0457 Hours

Mark had arrived more than an hour early and found the gate to the fire station locked. He had patiently sipped a Diet Coke and listened to the radio. After about fifteen minutes, one of the early rising firemen had come and unlocked the gate. He took advantage of the friendly, young man's offer of directions to the bathroom and continued to wait. The weather had changed, and the early morning sky was filled with stars. A slight sliver of a moon was setting just above the hills to the west. There was a December chill in the air and the slight breeze made it just a bit uncomfortable, despite the coat he wore over his uniform. He returned to his patrol car where he could take advantage of the heater. He tried to let his mind wander to PK, but for once, he was having a hard time finding her image in his mind. Instead, he was just a bit keyed up. He had never participated in a large search warrant. While he had some idea of what to expect, this was all new ground in his law enforcement career, and he didn't want to screw up. So he waited. At least he wouldn't be late.

After about another fifteen minutes, two dark colored SUVs pulled into the parking area of the fire station. Four men spilled out of the vehicles. He didn't recognize any of them, but they were wearing coats that had the word "POLICE" spelled out across the back. He shut off his car and braved the cold to introduce himself. He sized up the men and headed towards the one that appeared to be in charge. He was trying to read body language, but where all the men were Type A personalities,— as such, it was a bit hard. The men were joking amongst themselves and he was hesitant to intrude. However, the man that he thought was in charge saw him.

"You must be Mark Coltrane." The agent extended his right hand while speaking. "That was some good patrol work out there. I'm Agent Thorton and these fine gentlemen, the term used loosely of course, are Agents Thompson, Rickles, and Bach. This is Agent Mulhouse's investigation. He's running just a bit late. We're also expecting a couple of Sheriff's Deputies. We'll brief when everyone gets here. Hang out for a bit. Probably ought to use the pisser if you haven't already."

Agent Thorton returned his attention to the men he had arrived with. Mark tried to listen to their banter without appearing to eavesdrop, but he didn't know the people they were talking about, so most of the humor was lost on him. He decided to return to the warmth of his patrol car until more of the team showed up. The four agents also elected to seek shelter, with two heading towards the building housing the bathroom while the other two returned to their vehicle. He heard it start up, presumably so that they could run the heater also. He sipped his soda and waited, listening to the oldies radio station. At this rate, he was going to have to pee again.

At about ten minutes after six, two Sheriff's Department trucks pulled into the parking lot. Deputies spilled from these vehicles also. A third truck arrived a few minutes later, pulling a utility trailer hauling two ATVs. The last vehicle to arrive was a white, unmarked pickup driven by Agent Mulhouse. As Mulhouse got of his truck, the men began to gather in a circle. He joined the group, zipping up his coat and turning up the collar. It was still almost an hour to dawn, and air here was noticeably colder than closer to the coast.

"Good morning." Mulhouse began as several of the men returned his greeting as one handed him a cup of coffee. "The target of this morning's operation is a man named James Rickstraw. He is a documented Hells Angel member from the San Jose area. He has been in Big Tree County for about a month now. He has been trading meth for weed. Apparently, the weed market is something that his chapter, or at least portions of his chapter, would like to get into. He has been seeking out partners in the area." Mulhouse had used finger quotes around the word "partners" as he spoke. Mulhouse continued: "He has demanded twenty percent of the product from at least five growers in the Trout Creek area. Our targeted property is one of those growers, Sunshine Garvey. Garvey was stopped by Officer Coltrane in Small Town. Almost six ounces of meth and some weed were seized. Garvey claimed he got the meth from Rickstraw. He also claimed that Rickstraw was staying at his property and had about a pound more. Rickstraw is believed to be armed and should be considered dangerous."

With that, Mulhouse began to hand out documents. When Coltrane was handed one, he saw that it was the search warrant's Raid Plan. All of the officers participating were listed on the cover page, as well as their radio call signs and, in a few cases, mobile phone numbers. His name and call sign were included. *Cool*, he thought. As Mark flipped through the pages, he saw that there were pictures of Garvey, a tough looking man listed as James Rickstraw, and then aerial photographs of a clump of structures surrounded by woods. A dirt road accessed the structures, and he could make out a gate where the road exited the surrounding trees. He assumed that this was Garvey's property. He could also see trails that led from the complex into the woods behind the house, but it was not apparent what the trails led to as there was nothing visible but tree canopies. There were several vehicles parked in front of the largest of the structures. The aerial photographs were taken at an angle to the ground and he believed that they had been taken from a helicopter. Again, he thought this was pretty cool.

Mark returned his attention to Mulhouse as he began to speak again. "On page three of the briefing are pictures of Rickstraw and Garvey. Rickstraw has a conviction for robbery from 1984. He served six years in Quentin. Since then he has had a couple of arrests for drug sales, but no convictions. San Jose PD has him listed as a person of interest in a drug related homicide but doesn't have enough evidence yet to arrest him. If we can't arrest him, we'd like to encourage him to go back to San Jose. He is supposed to be driving a red Jeep Cherokee. Garvey, on the other hand, doesn't have much of a criminal history. He has a conviction for DUI from several years ago, but other than some minor traffic stuff, he has been flying under the radar. He's pretty squirrely though and I don't trust him not to do something really stupid if given half the chance. If we find probable cause to hook him up, I want him arrested even though he has been half-heartedly cooperating. He was stopped while driving a black '86 Toyota pickup."

Mulhouse continued the briefing. "On page four, there is a photograph of Garvey's property. Bach and I conducted a creep there two days ago. We were able to make it to where the road leaves the trees without being spotted. The structures were all dark. The only vehicles present were a silver Toyota pickup and an older Ford F150. There were at least two dogs outside, and since we didn't want to wake up whoever was there, we didn't try to circle the opening. We both thought we could hear a generator running, though. The parcels aren't real big in this area, so we weren't certain that the generator was on Garvey's property. We'll figure that out when we get out there and have some time to explore. Any questions so far?"

One of the deputies asked if they had been able to read the plates on the trucks. Agent Mulhouse responded, "There wasn't enough ambient light for my night scope to work at that distance. But Tara Garvey, Sunshine's wife, has a '79 Ford pickup registered to her and I think that was the older truck that was there. DMV says the family also owns a '91 BMW in addition to Garvey's pickup. We didn't see it there, but given the state of the road, they are probably using the old Ford to get through the mud and have the car parked much closer to pavement." Mulhouse looked around and didn't see any other questions. He then continued, "As far as we know, in addition to Rickstraw, Garvey and his wife, there are two children and an elderly man living in the main house. We don't think that anyone else will be on the property, but it is hard to say for sure. There are friends and relatives who visit from time to time. There is a shed behind the house that is occasionally used as a bedroom when the family has company. We think that is where Rickstraw is staying. There is a greenhouse about two-hundred feet to the north and a couple of small outbuildings in between. We don't expect to find any weed in the greenhouse this time of year, but you never can tell. Both Tara and Sunshine Garvey have multiple firearms registered to them.

And Rickstraw is supposed to carry a .45 with him all of the time. Are there any questions about the layout of the place?"

Seeing none, Mulhouse continued: "Ok, we'll run the op like this. Deputy Bishop will lead in his truck. The gate will take a torch to cut the lock off. It was locked on the creep. If it is still locked, we'll park at the gate and approach on foot. If it is open or dummy locked, we'll advance to the front of the main residence in vehicles. Bishop, have your lights on if we drive in. We'll try and stay stealthy if we go in on foot. It might still be a bit dark. Remember there are dogs, so have your pepper spray ready. Bishop and his partner, Bach, Rickles, and I will go to the rear of the residence and secure the shed first. We'll make entry to the main residence from the rear. Thorton and Thompson will establish a perimeter on the front of the main compound and secure anyone who comes out the front door. Deputy Clark and his partner will check the other outbuildings and the greenhouse to make sure that they are empty. Jackson, you and Coltrane will cut the lock on the gate and start to shuttle vehicles into the property if the gate is locked. If it is open, just follow us in and establish an outer perimeter. Primary communications will be on CLEMARS. The secondary radio frequency will Sheriff's Department D repeater. Any questions on the entry plan?"

Coltrane had lots of questions running through his mind, but since they didn't really deal with his assignment, he remained quiet. But he wondered how five men could enter and control such a large structure with so many people present, including one who was reported to be dangerous. And why do the service when the kids and other family members would be home? But they had done this kind of thing countless times before, so they should know their capabilities. He tried to refocus on the briefing as Mulhouse continued: "Once we get the structures secured, we will separate Rickstraw and bring the Garvey family into one of the main rooms in the house. We will reorganize at that point. The Sheriff's deputies can search the woods to the rear of the compound and see if they can locate the generator while the Task Force searches the house. If there aren't any questions, we'll pull out in ten minutes. Use the head and gear up now as we won't be stopping enroute."

Coltrane went over to Deputy Jackson and introduced himself. Jackson was an older man, a bit overweight perhaps, but still with a look of competency. He didn't seem to be perturbed by being assigned a tertiary role in the service of the search warrant. Coltrane thought about it and realized that his assignment made sense. These men worked and trained together on a regular basis. Throwing an unknown into the smooth working machine might bind up the cogs. Coltrane queued up for the bathroom and then returned to his vehicle to get his lunch and some additional drinks. He thought about grabbing his shotgun, but elected against it, given his role in the operation. When he was ready, he rejoined Jackson by his truck. Jackson had made room for him in the front seat. There was gear stacked in every nook, crook and cranny. He put his lunch at his feet and climbed in. He opened another Diet Coke, but couldn't find a place to put the bottle after taking a swig. He elected to stick it between his thighs. The great, or maybe not so great, adventure was about to begin.

They headed west towards the ocean, the last vehicle in a convoy of six. He had never been this way before. He had done some logging north of here, but never this far into SoCo. His occupation made sight-seeing here just a bit problematic, as he knew he and his kind were not overly welcome. The sun was still below the horizon, but the darkness was beginning to fade. He could see lights in the windows of many of the houses they passed. The community was just beginning to wake up. He also noticed that almost all of the driveways he saw had closed gates across them. They seemed to be more for security than to keep livestock contained, as he saw no cattle and only a few horses. *Life here was definitely different than in town*, he thought to himself.

Jackson was fiddling with the radio while sipping on a cup of coffee and steering along the winding road that made its way through the hills. They had crossed the river, travelled through a nice stand of old-growth redwood, but now they were in hills of mixed fir and grassland. The road rose, dipped, turned right and then left with abandon. Coltrane's stomach began to feel just a bit queasy. He rolled down the window just a crack. The cold air on his face made him feel a bit better. Jackson had found the radio station he was looking for and an eclectic collection of music filled the truck cab. He looked at Jackson. He seemed to easily tolerate his presence and he decided he would try and gain a better grasp on what was going on. It might be a long drive after all.

So he asked, "When Mulhouse said they did a creep, what does that mean?"

Jackson turned and looked at him briefly before returning his attention to the road. "So, the fucking new guy can speak. I wasn't sure there for a minute. So, you want to know about creeps? A creep is when these young bucks get out their military stuff and play soldier. They gear up with night vision goggles and rifles. An unmarked unit drops two or three members off in the wee hours of the morning, usually above the target so they can walk downhill. They move towards the intended target on foot while they hope everyone else is asleep. They cross fences and try to stay off of the roads as much as they can. Then they sneak around the target property as much as possible without getting detected.

It's pretty risky, but they can get good intelligence too. It's usually really quiet at three in the morning, so things like generators are pretty easy to find. They can also locate gates and other obstacles on the route in so that we can prepare for them in advance. The downside is that any confrontation is likely to be a bit ugly. In the dark, it's hard for anyone else to tell that they're cops and there are few legitimate reasons for guys to be wandering around the woods in the dark. The people down here are more afraid of being ripped off than they are of us. Consequently, they have a tendency to shoot first and begin to ask questions later. There is a reaction team in the drop off car in case the guys doing the creep run into trouble. But the idea is to get in and out without being seen. It usually works, but not always. We haven't had any shootings, but it has come close a couple of times. And the bad guys are starting to get the same kind of equipment, including surveillance cameras with passive IR sensors. There's a lot of money down here and the bad guys like their toys too. The agents can usually see the cameras with their goggles, but I think more than one warrant has been blown by a poorly done creep."

He had not heard of this and as he processed what he had been told, he asked a second question, "Don't they need a warrant to enter the property?"

Again, Jackson looked at him, this time with a kind a wry grin, "No, they don't need a warrant as long as they stay out of the curtilage of any residences, or at least don't gather any evidence inside of the curtilage. The courts have ruled that there is no expectation of privacy in an open field. So, they can climb all the fences they want, walk past No Trespassing signs, you name it. The bad guys hate it, but it's the law, at least for now."

They continued to chat about rural marijuana enforcement and Mark realized that he knew almost nothing about this type of work. Jackson had the radio turned down low, but all of sudden the music stopped, and the DJ's voice came through in a slightly excited tone. Jackson turned up the radio.

"We have just received information that a convoy of six marked and unmarked law enforcement vehicles is headed west on Cove Road. Their destination is unknown at this time, but as information continues to come in, we will pass it on. Now back to the music."

"Is that legal?" Coltrane asked.

"Well, if someone gets hurt, I think the Sheriff's Association would sue the shit out of them, but other than that, we just consider it another of the joys of working in this part of the world. They don't care much for anyone with a badge down here."

They turned off the paved road and onto a track full of gravel and puddles. Jackson stopped the truck briefly and shifted into four-wheel-drive before taking off after the other vehicles. Coltrane watched as splashes from the puddles landed on his window. They drove slowly as the trailer bounced from rut to rut. There was a fork in the road and here they caught up to the rest of the convoy, which had stopped briefly. When they continued, Jackson explained that the lead truck had to cut a lock. They passed through a now open gate and Coltrane saw two short pieces of chain that had a padlock in the middle connecting them together. Just inside of the gate, they passed two sedans that both had mud splatters on the fenders, but otherwise looked like relatively nice cars. Mark didn't know enough about cars to identify them. They wound through a stand of second growth fir, the trailer continuing to bounce. The road condition had deteriorated, and the windshield was beginning to get peppered by mud thrown up by the vehicle in front of them. Jackson turned on the windshield wipers and washer fluid squirted across the glass.

The mud smeared, but Jackson slowed, widening the distance between his truck and the one in front, and he continued to hit the washer fluid until the windshield was relatively clear. They continued, splashing through the mud and puddles for more than a mile and a half. The truck occasionally slid briefly, but Jackson was easily able to regain control. It looked like he had done this many times before.

Again, the music on the radio came to a sudden halt and the DJ's voice came through the speakers. "The convoy of six law enforcement Vehicles has turned from Cove Road onto Trout Road. They went right at the fork. If you live in that area, take whatever precautions you feel are appropriate. We will continue to update you on this law enforcement action as information comes in."

Jackson turned off the radio and stated, "We're almost there anyway."

They rounded a bend, and sure enough, the truck in front of them had stopped in the middle of the road. A voice came over the California Law Enforcement Mutual Aid Radio System, "The gate's locked, proceed to the target on foot."

Mark watched as the two deputies in the truck in front of them jumped out, rifles in hand, and jogged up the side of the road. Jackson got out and went to the toolbox mounted on the side of his truck. He removed a small acetylene cutting torch rig. Coltrane picked it up as Jackson started down the track at a more sedate pace than the other deputies. Mark followed. As he struggled with the torch, he could hear a familiar sound: a diesel engine revving followed by the clatter of moving tracks. Then the revolutions dropped, and the noise of the tracks stopped, only to have the process repeated over and over.

He found Jackson stopped in front of a gate. It was made from tubular steel, except for a tongue that had been inserted into a slot in a vertical tube attached to the opposite gate post. The padlock securing the gate was inside of the vertical tube and there was no way to get a pair of bolt cutters around it. Jackson took the cutting torch from him and set it on the ground near the gate post. He adjusted the valves on the two tanks, opened the valves on the torch, and then sparked the gas-oxygen mixture. He again adjusted the valves on the torch until he had a blue flame about six inches long. He donned a pair of welding goggles and then directed the flame into the slot in the tube. Sparks flew out of the bottom of the tube as he worked on the lock.

Mark looked up towards where he thought the house should be, but it was screened by a small clump of trees. He was able to see two figures approach a greenhouse off to the side. And then he noticed that the dozer sounds had changed. Instead of the back and forth of a working dozer, the machine was running full out with track noises, almost one continuous whir of sound. He wondered what the hell was going on, but his assignment was here, and he would just have to wait to find out. The noise of the dozer moved from right to left and began to fade as the machine moved further away from where he was standing.

And then his radio came to life again, "L31, we need the quads as soon as you can get them here."

Jackson clicked his mike and responded with a simple, "Roger." He then turned to Coltrane and told him, "See if you can move some of the trucks out of the way so that I can pull in as soon as possible."

Mark left him and went back towards Jackson's tuck. The main road had continued past the turnoff to Garvey's residence. The trucks had just stacked one behind the other as they came to a stop. He found the one closest to the intersection and tried the door. It was unlocked and the motor was running. He jumped in and drove it about 25 yards past the access to the Garvey residence. He then did the same with the next truck in line. It wasn't running, but the key was on the visor. He parked it behind the first. This cleared the area between Jackson's rig and the intersection. The next vehicle was a task force SUV. It was also running, and he backed it out to the main road and then parked it behind the two trucks. Jackson had the gate open by this time and had moved the lead truck through the gate and then pulled it to the side of the road on some grass. Coltrane followed it with another SUV. And then the path was clear. Jackson hustled back to his truck and drove through the gate, stopping in front of the house. Coltrane watched as two deputies quickly dropped the loading ramp and drove off on the ATVs. It looked like they were heading in the same direction that the dozer had gone. Coltrane stopped playing tourist and started to bring the trucks into the compound. Jackson helped him and before long, all of the vehicles were scattered around the front and sides of the house. Mulhouse came up to him and asked him to watch the suspects who had been detained and directed him toward the main house.

As he climbed the stairs, he noticed that the siding was unfinished and that there were nails visible. The siding was beginning to weather and he wondered how many more winters this place would make it through without some maintenance. The front door was wide open. He stepped into a living room. The walls were sheetrock, but they had not been taped, mudded or painted. Screwheads were visible, showing where the studs were. The walls were bare except for one panel of sheetrock, which was covered with crayon drawings. There was a wood stove in the center of the room, a couch and a recliner facing a large TV hooked to a VCR player. There was a stereo next to the TV and large floor speakers on either side. Tapes for both the video player and the stereo were scattered around the entertainment center. To the right was a breakfast bar, and behind it a kitchen with stainless steel appliances. To the left was a hallway that led into the rest of the house. There were no floor coverings, just plywood flooring. It was an interesting combination of high-priced gadgets with a house that had not been finished.

But what had really caught his attention when he came through the door were the three people sitting on the couch. There were two children, a boy of about eight and a girl of about ten. Both were wearing pajamas. The boy was trying to look brave, but it was obvious from the tears and snot on his face that until very recently, he had been crying. He could not tell if the girl was crying or not, as her face was buried into the woman who sat between them. She was about thirty with short brown hair. But he barely noticed that. What he noticed, what really caught his eye, were the blue eyes that locked on to him as soon as entered the room. They were the color of the sky in the high mountains, an intense bright blue. But the eyes were not filled with warmth, but rather with what he could only interpret as hate and scorn. He could not hold the gaze of her eyes, but he had also seen that she was only wearing a pair of panties. He forced himself to focus on her face. He knew that it was not uncommon when serving warrants in the early morning to catch people in various states of undress. But his department made a priority of getting them at least minimally clothed as soon the scene was secured. Apparently, these guys did things a bit different.

Jackson followed him through the door. When he saw the woman on the couch, he turned to the agent in the kitchen and bellowed, "Why the fuck doesn't this woman have some clothes on?" There wasn't an answer and Jackson moved quickly into the kitchen to discuss the matter further.

Coltrane stopped in front of her and dropped to one knee. He still focused on her face. "Madam, where can I find you some clothes?"

Those eyes and the shape of her face; if her hair was blonde, she would look like an older PK. Then a cold feeling started to grow in the pit of his stomach. She nodded with her head towards the hallway and stated in a voice low in volume, but thick with disgust, "My bedroom is at the end of the hall. There are some sweats in the dresser."

He then turned towards Jackson and the agent who were in a heated, but whispered conversation. "Hey, Jackson. I'm going to get this woman some clothes."

Jackson looked at him and quickly nodded his understanding. He headed down the hallway, passing two bedrooms and a bathroom. He entered the last room. It had actually been finished, and the walls were light purple in color. Landscapes, done in watercolors, adorned the walls and brought more color to the room. Some of them were pretty good. It looked like a woman's room; he didn't see any sign that a man shared it. He looked for the dresser and found it just to the left of the door. But before he could open a drawer, he saw the framed photograph on top. It was a family shot in an 8X10 simple wood frame. An older couple stood with a young woman on either side. One of the young women was obviously the woman in the living room. The cold feeling in his stomach became an iceberg. The other woman was younger, and her blonde hair was pulled back in a ponytail, but as he surmised, the familial similarity between PK and her sister was striking.

"Well shit!" emerged from his lips as he started to open drawers. He found one that was filled with neatly folded sweatshirts and pants. He grabbed the top one of each and returned to the living room. There he had the woman stand and turn so that she faced away from him. The boy started to cry again as the separation between mother and son grew. But she whispered something Mark could not understand, and the boy stopped crying. The girl just stared at him. Her eyes were only slightly paler than her mothers, but there was no less hatred there. He placed the clothes on the couch between the children. He then took off the handcuffs that secured the woman's hands behind her back. He couldn't help but notice the goose bumps that covered the woman's shoulders and arms. It was then that he realized that he was still wearing his coat and the temperature in the room was almost as chilled as the reception he had received. The woman reached down and quickly donned the clothes he had provided. She then returned her hands to the small of her back, but Mark had already moved towards the wood stove. When he saw her position, he just told her to sit down. She did so and was once again enveloped with a child on either side.

Mark reached the wood stove and opened the door. As he had suspected, the fire was dead, not even a remnant of the coals remained. He returned to the couch and again dropped to one knee, but this time he placed himself in front of the boy. The boy would not hold his gaze but continued to look at his mother.

Coltrane spoke softly to him, "Can you light a fire? It's cold in here and your mother and sister could use the warmth."

The boy didn't speak but looked at his mother again. She nodded at him and the boy scooted off of the couch and went to a stack of kindling next to the stove. He wadded up some newspaper and placed it with what looked like dryer lint in the center of the firebox. He then stacked kindling above the tinder in a teepee shape. He stuck a match and lit the paper. Soon flames were licking the kindling and he started to add larger pieces of softwood to the fire. Within five minutes, a pretty good blaze was going in the firebox. The boy added a couple of large pieces of madrone on either side of the kindling fire and watched as they also started to burn.

The boy turned towards Coltrane and stated in a soft voice, "I have to leave the door open until the madrone catches." He put a third piece of hardwood across the other two, then rejoined his family on the couch, confident that the fire would continue without any more assistance from him.

Coltrane checked the videos on the shelf next to the TV. He then looked at the kids on the couch. "Would you guys like to watch something on TV?" Both children looked a bit confused but turned their attention to their mother. Once again, she nodded. Mark looked at the girl and asked, "You want to pick something?" The girl quickly went to the shelf holding the tapes, selected one, removed it from the sleeve and inserted it into the player. She hit a couple of buttons on the remote and the booming refrain from *The Circle of Life,* came through the speakers. The girl returned to the couch and cuddled with her mother. Coltrane found a blanket behind the sofa and helped the mother spread it across the three bodies. He noticed that the kid's eyes were transfixed on the TV, but the mother was still watching him. The hate that he had seen in her eyes had dissipated. But it had been replaced by a wariness that may have included a bit of fear. He guessed this was better, but he wasn't sure.

He squatted down for a third time so that he was at the same level as the detainees on the couch. As the movie's refrain ended, he started to speak, "I don't think we were properly introduced. My name is Mark. What are your names?"

The young boy erupted with, "My name is Mark too."

The girl, however, was either too shy or too well indoctrinated at this early age to give the cops any information. Instead, she just looked at him with those blue eyes and then turned her attention back to the movie. He turned his gaze to the woman. "Are you Tara?" She nodded in the affirmative. He then added, "I apologize for earlier this morning. I'll try to make our presence here as low key as I can. Have the kids had anything to eat yet this morning?" She shook her head in the negative. "Is there cereal or something else quick and easy?"

She spoke for only the second time, "There's raisin bran in the cupboard next to the fridge. The bowls are to the left of the sink and the silverware is in the top drawer." Gone was the tone of disgust. Instead, it had been replaced with a wary inquisitiveness, "Why are you doing this?"

He didn't know if she was referring to the invasion of her home by armed men or the kindness he was trying to project, but he elected to answer the latter and leave the other alone, "Because I believe in treating people as humans until they convince me that they are not."

He went into the kitchen, located the cereal, filled two bowls, added milk and grabbed a pair of spoons. He brought the breakfast back into the living room and handed a bowl to each child. But rather than beginning to eat, they both looked at their mother. She looked at them in kind and softly stated, "We'll make an exception today, go ahead and eat." She then looked at Mark and explained, "They're not allowed to eat in the living room."

"Can I get you something, coffee maybe?" Mark asked. But she shook her head in the negative. The kids' attention had already returned to the TV, but Tara's eyes followed him as he returned to the kitchen. He liked the feel of this kitchen. Unlike the living room, the floor was tiled, and the walls were painted a creamy white. A trellis covered with flowers had been painted around the opening to the living room and around the back door. More watercolors were on display. There were windows on three sides that let in the slowly increasing, morning light. A small table and two chairs sat next to the back door. There was ample counter and storage space. This was a room that was meant to be used. But it was also a room that was enjoyable to occupy. And he had noticed the discrepancy between the common areas of the house and those that belonged to Tara. He wondered what the kids' rooms looked like. He guessed that they too were filled with art, color, and light. This family was a conundrum wrapped around an enigma. In his own way, he admired Tara. She had shown nobility in the face of severe adversity. She had spoken her disdain with an unmatched eloquence and without a spoken word. He wished, he truly wished, that he could have met this woman in different circumstances, perhaps around a Christmas dining table. Instead, as he glanced around the kitchen one last time, he imagined Tara and PK sitting at the small table, sipping coffee. There wasn't room for him to join them. As he returned his gaze to the family on the couch, the cold lump in his stomach became an ache in his heart.

Chapter Fourteen

Garvey Compound

December 17, 1996, 0803 Hours

Mark watched the family from the kitchen. The fire had taken and the room was getting warmer. The kids were concentrated on the movie. Tara watched her children, watched him, and at times, seemed lost in thought. He and his fellow officers had definitely ruined their day, and maybe more than that. Christmas was not that far away. Would the family to be together for the holidays? After about a half hour, he went into the living room and gathered the cereal bowls when they were finally empty. And he stood, feeling pretty useless and unwanted.

Jackson came back to the main house a short time later. He briefed him on what had transpired so far. A man, presumed to be Garvey, had been running a dozer when they arrived. When he spotted the officers approaching the rear of the house, he stopped what he was doing and took off on the dozer. Two deputies gave chase on foot but were no match for the machine going uphill and cross country. They had found the dozer abandoned at the edge of a stand of timber. There was a road about 100 yards up the hill and through the trees. The deputies on the ATVs had been able to navigate between the trees, but very slowly. They had reached the road and had resumed the search, looking for footprints in the mud. Two more deputies had taken a truck and were trying to reach the same section of road to help. Consequently, they were short-handed here at the house and things were taking longer than anticipated. There had been no sign of Rickstraw, and there was some concern as to whether he had ever been here at all. The agents had found a diesel-powered generator grow just inside of the trees across the meadow from the house. Jackson agreed to relieve him if he wanted to go check it out, as it was apparent from the ride in that Mark had never seen this kind of marijuana cultivation.

Mark walked out the kitchen door. Right behind the house he found a shed. There was a faint odor of urine in the air. One of the agents had stapled a sheet of paper with a large D on it to the side of the shed next to the door, which was open. Mark poked his head inside. The room was a mess. There was a small woodstove in the center, and on one side of the small room was a stained mattress on the floor. A sleeping bag was lying on top of the mattress. Beer cans and dirty clothes were scattered throughout the rest of the room. The walls were covered with posters of scantily clad women selling products, primarily beer. A bong, along with a zip-lock bag of weed, sat next to the mattress. A pump-action shotgun was in close proximity. And as he looked closer, he could see a couple of small Ziplock bags that held only the remains of the methamphetamine that had once filled their void. These were commonly called scrapper bags in his world. The room didn't remind him of a hardened criminal, but of a tweaker. He wondered if this was Rickstraw's room, or was it Sunshine Garvey's? Garvey didn't sleep in his wife's room that was for sure.

He followed a path past the shed and across the meadow, and after about twenty-five yards, it forked. On the lower, right-hand side he saw dozer tracks. He took that path. He walked for about five minutes, following the tracks,. He came to a spot where it looked like the dozer had been working. The path had been widened out to almost twenty feet. Some of the soil had been cast over the side of the hill, but there was a large pile of loose soil right where the trail had been enlarged. The outer edges of the pile were almost straight up and down. It looked to Coltrane like Garvey had been using the dozer to push soil away from where he was standing, and from both sides of the pile. He thought that was a bit unusual and walked around the pile to get a better look at the work area. He noticed that there was a depression in the relatively level area behind the dirt pile. It was only a few inches deep, but about twenty feet long and maybe seven feet wide. It looked like Garvey may have been filling in a large hole in the ground and that he was doing it from both sides, as the depression was deeper in the center and there was looser soil there then on the edges, for it had not been run over by the dozer's tracks. He didn't know what to make of this but thought about it as he walked on. And then he noticed where the dozer tracks left the trail and went straight up the hill. He followed the tracks. The slope wasn't real steep, only about twenty percent (a twenty foot rise over one hundred horizontal feet). But even so, he was beginning to breathe hard when he came to the other trail. The tracks crossed right over the trail and continued up the hill. Mark followed. After about ten more minutes of cross-country walking, he came to the dozer. It was still running.

He examined the machine. It appeared to be the same type of dozer that he had run the most when he worked in the woods, a Cat D6D. He climbed into the operator's seat. The blade had been lowered and the throttle reduced to an idle, but the transmission was still in gear and the brakes weren't engaged. He locked both brakes and pushed the hand throttle to the off position. The muted roar of the engine ceased. He then twisted the ignition key to the off position and climbed back down to the ground. He started to retrace his steps, but before he was more than twenty yards from the dozer, Agent Mulhouse came out of the trees and hailed him. He turned back towards the narcotics officer who was walking towards him.

"Do you know how to run that thing?" Agent Mulhouse asked.

"It's pretty much the same machine I ran in the woods just a couple of years ago. You want me to move it somewhere?" he answered.

"Yeah, I think we are going to seize it as asset forfeiture. Can you drive it down to the area around the house? We'll figure out if we are going to take it a little later."

Mark climbed back into the operator's chair. He knew that a dozer, also commonly called a Cat after the major manufacturer, Caterpillar, was steered by the use of clutches and brakes on each track. To make a right turn, for example, you would pull the right friction lever which disengaged the clutch on the right track and as you pulled harder, engaged a brake on the same track. This caused the right side of the machine to slow while the left side was still moving at speed. The machine would then turn to the right. Another one of the other major differences between this machine and a car was that the throttle was a hand lever that was almost always in one of three positions, off, full throttle, or idle. A decelerator was mounted on the floor and controlled by the right foot. As you pressed on this pedal, the engine's RPMs decreased rather than increased.

Mark flipped the ignition back to the on position and pulled the throttle to idle. As the machine was still warm, it started right up with a bellow of exhaust when he hit the starter button. He stepped on the decelerator and then pulled the throttle all the way towards him. He used another lever on the right side of the seat to raise the blade, released the brake lock and shifted the automatic transmission into reverse. The machine started to roll backwards as he released pressure on the brake. He then pulled the left friction lever as he eased up on the decelerator and the rear of the machine started to swing to the left. When he had the machine pointed in the right direction, he released the friction lever, pushed the decelerator to the floor, and shifted into second gear. The dozer took off as he eased up on the brake and decelerator. He cruised back down to the trail, where he slowed to just a crawl as he went over the cut-slope. He raised the blade as high as it would go so that it wouldn't dig into the ground when he came to the change of slope. He then turned and followed the trail back towards the house. It felt good to be back in charge of the immense power that these machines possessed. He parked the dozer by the side of the house and went to find Jackson.

Jackson was inside of the house with the family. He had made himself a cup of coffee and was watching the end of the *Lion King* with the kids. Tara still appeared to be remaining as silent as she could be. He asked Jackson if he had a shovel in his truck, and Jackson looked at him with a questioning glance, but confirmed that he did and told him where to find it. Mark returned to Jackson's truck, found the shovel and started walking back towards where the dozer had been working. He might be making a fool of himself, but he was pretty curious about what Garvey had been doing It looked like he was burying something rather large.

As he walked past the pile of dirt, he examined the depression in the ground one more time. Garvey had been working from the sides to fill the hole, rather than from the ends which would have been easier and more efficient. There was no indication that he had actually driven the dozer into the depression. This made Mark think that whatever he was burying might not support the weight of the dozer. He went to the center of the depression, where he figured that the soil layer was the thinnest. He pushed the shovel blade in and started to dig. He didn't hit anything with the first few efforts, but he persisted. The soil was heavy with moisture, so it was hard work. After about fifteen minutes, the hole was about eighteen inches deep and two feet wide. He placed the shovel blade at the center of the hole and stepped down on it. It went in about five inches and hit something hard. He moved over about six inches and tried the same thing with the same result. He smiled to himself; there was something buried here. He continued to dig. When the hole was about two feet deep and three feet around, he got down on his knees and started to wipe the mud away from the buried object with his gloved hands. He was rewarded with the sight of a concave red surface. He went back to work with the shovel and in about another ten minutes, he had a clearer picture. It appeared that he had uncovered the roof of a red vehicle that had been collapsed by the weight of the soil on top of it. The top of a broken windshield was just visible at the edge of the hole.

He looked at the raid plan that he had put in a thigh pocket. "Nora 81, A15, I think I have something you might want to take a look at. I'm at the dirt pile on the lower trail."

After a short pause, he heard "Roger A15, ETA is about ten minutes."

He sat down to catch his breath. When Agent Mulhouse arrived, Mark showed him what he had found. Mulhouse also recognized what he had uncovered, and his response was a simple, "Oh shit!" He hurried back to the house. Mark sat back down on the pile of dirt. Mulhouse returned in about fifteen minutes with Agent Thornton. They both looked in the hole at the top of the vehicle.

Thornton said, "I'll call and see if we can get an excavator out here, but that probably won't happen until tomorrow. Have you called for detectives yet?"

Mulhouse answered, "No, I want to find out more information before I cry wolf. Is there any way we can dig down by hand to see if there is anything inside? Like a body?"

Thornton looked at Mulhouse with a look that was part disbelief and part humor. "Knock yourself out kid."

Then Mulhouse looked at Coltrane, "Can you dig this thing out with the Cat?"

Mark paused before answering, "I'm pretty rusty when it comes to moving dirt, but I could probably dig out enough soil on the downhill side so that you could use a shovel to uncover the windows. It would at least give you some idea of what was buried there and maybe get a look inside. Do you think it's Rickstraw's Jeep?"

Thornton answered, "That's my fear, that and his body might be inside of it. If that's the case, we'll be here for days."

Mark walked back to the house and fired up the Cat again. He walked it back to the burial site, maneuvered around the dirt pile and went further up the hill past where they thought the car was buried. There he turned around. He wanted gravity working on his side. He parked and got down. He looked the ground over, forming a plan. Then he took the shovel he had used to unearth the top and stuck it in the ground at the edge of the depression.

"What's that for?" Thornton asked.

"I'm going to use it as a grading stake. When I start to get real close to it, I'm going to stop and use it to see how far from the car I am."

"Sounds like a plan," Thornton simply replied.

And with that, Mark began the process. He backed a little further up the hill, lowered the blade and put the dozer into gear. As he let up on the decelerator, soil began to curl up in front of the blade. When the tracks began to spin, he raised the blade slightly, pulled the left friction lever, and pushed the accumulated loose soil over the bank. He repeated the process again and again. His first few passes were slow and kind of clumsy. But the muscle memory returned, and the passes grew in both speed and efficiency. A new trail was being created that paralleled the first but was lower. He worked to make the cutslope of this second trail closer to the upended shovel. After about thirty minutes of steady work, the shovel toppled as he was backing up for another pass. There was a drop of about five feet between the two trails. He parked the machine, got down, and gathered the shovel.

He began to dig away at the almost vertical bank. He used gravity to pull the soil down with the shovel. Within only a few minutes he had unearthed what was clearly the side of a red vehicle. He continued to work with the shovel and increased the area that was visible. First it was a crumpled roof, then a door post that had buckled inward. He continued to work by hand. The sun was getting higher in the sky and he paused to take off his jacket. He could feel the moisture in his undershirt as his muscles loosened and he began to sweat. *Sometimes, no matter how far you move forward in life, you take some backward steps,* he thought as he remembered how much this work mirrored his previous career in the woods.

Thornton disappeared, but came back with another shovel. Mulhouse just continued to watch as the side of a partially crushed Jeep Cherokee began to take form. Thornton started to work on the front of the vehicle while Mark worked on the rear. Between the two men, it didn't take too much longer before the side of the car was exposed to the wheels. The side windows had all broken from the pressure of the crumpled roof. Thornton cleared the soil away from the driver's side front window, and in doing so, he inadvertently pushed some soil into the cabin, but he could now see in. Mark handed him a small flashlight from his duty belt. Thornton examined the inside of the vehicle for more than a minute. Mark could see the light beam move around the inside of the buried vehicle.

Thornton backed away finally and stated, "Well, it could be worse." He handed the light back to Mark and started to clear away the soil from the next window in line. Mark moved to the driver's side and looked through what remained of the window. The gap was only about a foot high, but he could see the interior. At first, he didn't see anything that looked amiss. But he noticed that there were two holes in the black leather upholstery of the driver's seat. Then he looked at the remains of the windshield. Unlike the side windows whose safety glass had crumbled, the windshield was still in one piece, although the glass was shattered. However, just in front of the steering wheel, he saw two small holes in the glass. He studied the cracks radiating out from these holes and saw that these breaks in the glass continued for more than a foot from each hole. The other cracks in the glass stopped at these breaks. He remembered from a training class sometime in the past that this suggested that the radiating cracks from the holes had come first. He then compared the holes in the glass to the holes in the seat. They could be in line if whatever generated them came from slightly above. He looked into the rear of the vehicle but could not see anything of interest. He looked closer at the holes in the fabric. He didn't want to reach into the vehicle as it was likely a crime scene, but it looked like he could see a kind of rust-brown discoloration of the black leather around the holes.

Mark backed away from the vehicle and then handed the flashlight to Thornton. He had cleared the soil away from the remaining two windows on this side of the Jeep. The rear of the SUV had been crushed down further than the front, but it was still possible to look inside. Thornton turned on the light and peered inside. He didn't spend as much time as he did in the front.

"No sign of a body," he said with relief. "But we had better call for some detectives. It looks like it might be a crime scene."

Thornton turned and walked towards the house to make the phone call.

Mark stood by the side of the vehicle, not sure what to do next. But Jackson walked up within seconds and signaled for Mark to follow him. They walked past the buried car and followed the trail towards the forest across the meadow. Just inside of the tree cover, Jackson pointed to a hole in the bank that was fortified with sandbags. Another sheet of paper with a large N printed on it was attached to one of the bags.

Jackson explained what he was looking at, "They took a Conex box and buried it in the hillside. This is their generator room. They cut a hole in the back of the container to vent the exhaust. Go check it out."

Mark took out his flashlight again and ducked his head to enter the container. It was a standard short container, twenty feet long and eight feet wide. He shone the light around the inside. There was a large diesel-powered generator in the center. He could see 45 kW written in black on the machine's orange paint. It was running, making a loud humming sound. He walked towards the rear of the container. Against the back wall were at least ten, five-gallon buckets. He looked inside and saw that they contained what looked to be waste oil. He slipped slightly and looked down at the floor of the container. He noticed that it, too, was covered with a thin sheen of oil. He grimaced slightly and cautiously retraced his steps. He saw a thin, plastic line run into the fuel tank of the generator, and several electrical lines run from the output of the machine into a conduit that then went underground by the door. What appeared to be the fuel line entered the container from a hole just above the generator. A large, silver, flexible pipe about eighteen inches in diameter, led the exhaust from the machine through another hole at the back of the container.

He returned to the sunlight and found that Jackson had disappeared. He walked up the hill and found where the fuel line ran across the ground. As he continued up the hill, he saw where the exhaust vented at ground level. There were fewer leaves and forest debris around the large hole in the ground, but the area had not been raked clean in some time. The freshly fallen leaves were singed black from the heat and soot, and he could only imagine the fire risk in the summertime. He followed the fuel line up the hill. After walking about 200 yards, he saw the other trail through the trees. He had not walked it out to the end, being sidetracked by the dozer tracks going up the hill. He continued to follow the fuel line and found that it terminated at four large, rust-brown colored tanks that had been laid on the gently sloping ground. He did some calculations in his head: four feet in diameter and about twelve feet long meant each tank had a volume of about 145 cubic feet or a little over a 1000 gallons per tank. The valves for the tanks were on the down-hill side and were all connected together by one line, similar to the one he had followed, only slightly larger. That line then merged into the fuel line that headed down the hill to the generator. The smell of diesel was strong in the cold air, and as he looked closer, he could see fuel gather and then drip from the connections to the feeder line. He checked the soil under all of the valves and found that it also smelled strongly of diesel fuel. He had seen some pretty bad environmental practices when he worked in the woods, and this was no better. He continued up the hill the short distance to the trail. There were dual tire tracks in the wet soil that he had not seen during his walk; he had only really been paying attention to the dozer tracks. The tire tracks were not fresh, but had not been washed away entirely by the recent rains either. A fuel delivery must have taken place not that long ago. Just past the fuel tanks the trail had been widened out significantly. It was clear from the tire tracks that this area was used by the fuel truck to turn around. He walked to the edge of this small, level pad. Just beyond the furthest edge about five feet, ran a small creek. The water ran over small stones interspersed with tanoak leaves. He was confident that the stream was ephemeral, only running in the winter and maybe only after storm events, but the channel was awfully close to where diesel fuel was steadily leaking onto to the ground.

He turned around and retraced his steps to the buried generator. He tried to follow the electrical lines, but they did not resurface outside of the container. He looked across the trail into the trees. Everything was in shadows and it was only when Jackson opened a door to one of the grow rooms that Mark could make it out. Jackson was backlit by a harsh orange light. The door was at the end of a building painted a drab green with black and brown camouflage applied to it. He had looked right at it and not seen the structure. It was about eight feet wide and maybe forty feet long. As his eyes become accustomed to what to look for, he saw that there were additional grow rooms below and further along the trail. Some were wider and some were longer. All of them seemed to be of a simple construction with plywood siding and a post and pier foundation. Again, Jackson beckoned him to follow.

He entered the room and saw that there was a path about a foot wide between two raised beds that occupied the rest of the room. Grow lights hung from the ceiling and extension cords crisscrossed above his head. Ventilation fans were mounted on the walls. The raised beds were filled with marijuana plants, most of which were about two feet high and crowded together so that their canopies overlapped. The plants were just beginning to develop buds. Towards the far end of the room was another door. Just inside of that door was a plastic tank that held a greenish colored fluid. He asked Jackson what the fluid was, and he learned that it was fertilizer mix. A garden hose with a sprinkler head lay haphazardly in the middle of the path between the two beds. Another hose, albeit smaller, was attached to the fertilizer tank.

Jackson came up to him and handed him a pair of pruning shears. "While you were busy playing in the dirt, we photographed and diagramed all of these grow rooms and now we're ready to start cutting. Count each plant you cut. When you get done, give me the number and we'll move the plants to the path where they can be picked up."

Mark bent down and started to cut marijuana plants he found in the cramped space. He moved towards the back of the building while Jackson worked towards him on the other side. When he got to the end, he had counted 453 plants. He gave this number to Jackson who wrote it down on a sheet of paper with a large S printed on it. They then gathered up the cut plants and started to carry them out the door and dump them in the trail. The plants were still several weeks from harvest, but they did have some resin on their buds, and it did not take long before Mark's uniform was covered in the sticky substance. He wondered what Gunner would think of this new smell he brought home from work.

When they finished the first grow room they moved to a second. It was wider, but otherwise similar in design and function to the first. He noticed that two of the agents were also processing additional grow buildings. When he was done with his half of this room, he added another 685 plants to the tally. His back ached from all of the groundwork and his feet were getting tired. He and Jackson met up with the other agents. He learned that one of the grow buildings had contained a nursery with mother plants and about 2000 clones. Almost 1800 budding plants had been brought out to the path for disposal. The baby clones and the mother plants, which weren't allowed to bud, had been cut and left behind. One of the agents returned to the grow rooms to take an additional set of pictures, while he and Jackson sat down on the edge of the trail, soaking up some of the early afternoon sun.

Mark asked him, "What's going to happen with all of the environmental damage that's going on here?"

"We've called Fish and Game. They will send a warden out here. He'll likely submit a report to the District Attorney's Office. The criminal charges won't amount to much, but if the right Deputy DA gets the case, they may make the owner clean up the mess he has created. But it is more likely that about a week after we leave, they will be back in business. That's kind of the way it works."

Jackson paused briefly and then continued, "We would normally try and take the generator as part of asset forfeiture, but since this one is buried, we're not going to do that. The lights and ballasts are considered hazardous waste and are really expensive to get rid of. We used to seize them, but the cost became prohibitive. None of the structures get destroyed, and the beds are still there waiting to be replanted. We set them back a growing cycle and cost them a considerable amount of money, but didn't really do much damage to their operation. It's all just part of the game."

Mark didn't understand, "What do you mean by game?"

Jackson smiled, "Sometimes ignorance is bliss. It's a game. The grower's goal is to make as much money as possible, ours is to pretend to try and stop them. The powers that be don't really want the marijuana money to stop coming into the County. It's what drives the economy here. So, we come out a couple of times a week in the summer, less in the winter, and we cut a bunch of plants. We make life uncomfortable for a day, and then we're gone. We generate fear— fear of being raided, fear of prosecution, fear of the unknown. This keeps the number of growers at a reasonable level. If there was no fear, the number of growers would sky-rocket and the price would tumble. The locals don't really want that. So, they tolerate our raids, sort of anyway. We keep the price of weed up. If we start to get too successful, they use their political clout to reign us in. They're good at that. The Sheriff is an elected official; he listens when they complain. The Board of Supervisors are their friends. Then the rules change slightly in their favor, but we find other ways to do business. Technology improves and gives us new advantages, and the game goes on; nothing really changes. The fear continues, the money flows in. They hate us because we scare them. We're contemptuous because of the money they make and their lack of respect for authority, including ours. It's just a game. Well, at least until someone gets hurt, it's just a game. I'll get off my soapbox now."

Mark thought about this for a moment. He could see Jackson's point. He kind of considered his job a game. The laws were the rules. His goal was to harass the troublemakers in town to the point where they left for another location, somewhere the cops weren't as aggressive. The bad guys' goal was to make him look as stupid as possible. He won more encounters than he lost. But there was little in the way of reformation in his goals. If that was to occur, it would be the result of a decision made by those who needed reforming. All he could do was try to make their lives miserable and in so doing, to help them come to that decision.

And after all that thinking, Mark laid his head back on the grass and was asleep within seconds.

Chapter Fifteen

Garvey Compound

December 17, 1996, 1128 Hours

A dirt-clod skidded across his chest and Mark came awake with a start. He saw Jackson readying another missile to gain his attention.

"Hey, Sleeping Beauty. Mulhouse wants you at the house," Jackson told him. Mark looked at his radio, but Jackson added, "I took care of that for you. Just get going."

So, he got up off the ground. His lack of sleep was catching up with him and he realized that he was more tired that he thought. He began the trudge down the trail to the house, and wondered what they wanted him for.

As he approached the back of the Garvey's house, he saw a person he had not met yet standing next to Thorton. She had a feminine figure, was of average build, had dirty blonde hair worn in a ponytail extending out of the back of a baseball cap, and she was wearing a green jacket that read "SHERIFF" on the back. She turned to face him. He could see that the woman was younger than he was by at least five years. Awfully young to be a detective, he thought to himself. She had rather plain features except for her eyes. They were hooded and intense, almost hawk like. Mark thought that they contrasted with the rest of her face, which was warm and welcoming. They were joined by another man. He was older, with salt and pepper hair, a mustache that was mostly gray, and a scowl that suggested that he would rather be someplace else. He too, was wearing a green jacket that covered most of the pistol he wore holstered on his belt. The detectives had arrived.

Thorton spoke first, "Officer Coltrane, this is Sergeant Shawn Grady and Detective Ericka O'Rourke. They're here to help figure out what happened to Rickstraw. You're going to be assisting Detective O'Rourke with interviewing the woman inside. Sergeant Grady is going to help us take a look at the vehicle you unearthed."

Coltrane was puzzled. "Why do you want me to help interview Tara? This isn't my jurisdiction, this isn't my case. Shouldn't someone else be doing that?" he asked.

"Well," Grady started in a gruff, slow drawl, "Because she swears that she is only going to talk to you and even some gibberish might be better than nothing." He turned his back and walked off in the direction of the path that led to the buried Jeep. Mulhouse and Thorton followed him.

He turned to O'Rourke. "Your partner is not in the best of moods, but I do appreciate his vote of confidence."

Her face lit up again with another smile and even her eyes danced a bit. "He had plans to go fishing today, but we got called out before he got out of his driveway. His normal partner is away at training and the only detective left was me. He doesn't like me very much. He didn't speak five words on the two hours it took to get here, and I drove pretty fast. Then your girlfriend in there pretty much told him to fuck off and that she would only talk to you. I'm guessing that his blood pressure is soaring. So be thankful that you're stuck with me and not having to deal with his sniping for the rest of the day."

He entered the house through the kitchen door and was just a bit surprised to see Tara sitting at the small table just inside the door instead of on the couch. She had a coffee cup in her hands and a saucer sat in front of her. She turned as he entered, and he thought he saw a hint of a smile forming on her lips and around her eyes before her mouth opened and words ushered forth. "My savior has returned." The words were rich with sarcasm, but he wondered that if deep down, she didn't feel just a bit relieved to see him.

His response was also heavily laden with sarcasm and it surprised him just a bit that he was confident enough to say, "I love you too." But again, it was if the words and the inflection did not matter; they were speaking with their facial expressions rather than their vocal cords. For he had smiled as he spoke, and the smile was genuine. And he just might love her sister, so it wasn't really all that much of a stretch.

But instead of stopping in the kitchen, Mark continued into the living room. The kids were still huddled on the couch, wrapped in a blanket, and with their eyes glued to the tube. He went to the rear of the room and turned to face O'Rourke. "How do you want to handle this?" he asked.

"Well, what I learned in detective school was to initially just talk; try and build some rapport. You seem to already have that, but I would recommend going slow at the start and see what happens. She won't talk to me either, so I am just going to take notes. I'll kick you though if I think you are screwing up."

"How many times have you done this?" he asked.

"This is my first case that isn't child abuse," was her answer. "I have only been in Investigations for about a month. That's one of the reasons that Grady has some serious heartburn."

He smiled at her and led the way back into the kitchen. He took the chair opposite from Tara. He wanted to be on the same level, to be able to look directly into her eyes. He wasn't sure if he could tell if she was telling the truth or not, but he thought it was worth making O'Rourke stand. That and he didn't want to be perceived as coming from a place of dominance.

And so he began: "Tara, my name is Mark Coltrane. I'm a police officer in Small Town. About a week and a half ago, I stopped your husband on the freeway north of town. He had a warrant for his arrest on a very minor charge. When I took him into custody, I found about six ounces of methamphetamine in addition to several pounds of marijuana and a loaded revolver. I turned him over to the Drug Task Force. Your husband told them about James Rickstraw and his attempts to extort money from some of the growers in this area. They prepared a search warrant to try and catch Rickstraw on your property. Unfortunately, he does not appear to be here. Instead, it looks like he might have fallen prey to some type of foul play. The Task Force called in detectives to try and figure where what happened to Rickstraw. And since you refused to speak with Sergeant Grady or anyone else about this matter, I am sitting before you. Detective O'Rourke is going to assist me by taking notes. You are not under arrest and you can end this interview at any time you want. You are not free to leave the house, however. In addition, I would appreciate it if you told me the truth. If you don't want to answer a question, simply say so and I'll move on. But please, don't feed me a line of bullshit. Do you understand the situation?"

She responded by nodding her head. Mark decided to forge on without an audible response. "You have a nice place here. But I can't help but noticing the discrepancy in the rooms of your house. Tell me about your life and how you came to live here?"

Tara looked at him with some puzzlement. She was silent for a time and he wondered if he had asked too much in one question. She tilted her head to the side, much like her sister did. Mark imagined the gears turning in her head and was preparing a more focused follow-up question, when she elected to respond: "This land belonged to Sunny and his family. I have known Sunny for years, as my family owns property across the canyon. But we only got married two years ago. He is not the father of my children; Svetlana is the product of a one-night stand and Mark's father died in a crash out in the cove when Mark was just a baby. My family helped me raise my children and we were loved and cared for. Then Sunny came back from an extended trip to Mexico. He swept me off my feet, showing both the children and me more attention than we were accustomed to. I agreed to marry him and move here. He built us this house. But then, then he found meth. Sunny, like almost everyone out here, was a farmer. We used to grow what we needed to get by and not much more, food, gas, a roof over our head, and a Winter trip to somewhere warm. But he met some people in Mexico that talked him into a bigger scene. They financed the diesel grow in the trees. And with that came money, lots of money. Sunny had never had a lot before. He didn't know what to do with it all. So, he experimented with all kinds of things, some good and some not so good. Guns, girls, cars, and drugs were what he ended up with. He liked cocaine, he liked meth, and he had the money to buy whatever he wanted. And so, his life was consumed by drugs; his family became a sideshow. He wasn't a strong man. It wasn't much of a battle."

She continued: "He stopped working on the house completely and started to spend more and more time in town and in the Bay Area. He met new people, people with different values. I worked on the house while he was gone. I finished the bedrooms and the kitchen but ran out of money. When Sunny started the indoor operation, I continued to grow flowers in the greenhouse. I made enough money to get by, but not enough for more building supplies. When he gave me chlamydia, I kicked him out of the house, and he moved into the shed. He's only here occasionally these days and he's usually high as a kite when he is. I don't know what he was doing, but he was running the Cat all night long."

"I suppose I deserved a long answer to a complex question. I'm sure Erika is cursing me as she tries to keep up," was Mark's attempt at levity. He wanted to lighten the mood just a bit. "You mentioned your family with the words 'love and care'. Would you mind telling me about them? It might be easier than talking about Sunny."

She looked at him with some concern and her eyes focused on his. "Why do you want to know about my family?" she asked.

Well, there was more than one answer to that question he thought to himself. But he really had no choice in how to answer. "I asked you to be honest, so I guess that it is only fair that I am honest with you. I am trying to get to know you, learn a little bit about how you think. And I am trying to get you comfortable in answering my questions. If I ask non-invasive questions now, I can try and get you in the habit of answering. I am hoping that when I start to ask more difficult questions, you will continue to answer. So far, I think I am failing badly, what do you think?"

He watched the smile grow around her mouth and eyes as she gathered her thoughts. He could feel O'Rourke tapping against the back of his chair. But he still thought that he had read this woman right, that he needed to be honest with her, maybe excessively honest if he wanted to get anywhere. He based this in part on the direct, matter of fact way her sister asked questions. Tara was smart and would see through him if he tried to be deceptive or did not answer her questions. And then any chance of gaining information would be gone. Or at least, so he thought.

She continued to smile at him with her eyes as she began to speak. "I think you are smarter than you give yourself credit for. And I think you are doing quite well. What do you want to know about my family?"

"Whatever you want to tell me."

"I grew up nearby, where is not important. I lived with my parents, my younger sister, and my grandfather. It was a good family life. We had what we needed, and we shared a lot of love. My grandfather still spends most of the day with me. He sits on the porch and whittles most of the time. He would have been here today if it were not for you and your friends. I am sure that the word of your visit reached him long ago."

"Tell me about a childhood memory, first thing that pops into your head."

Her eyes smiled again. "You're not what I expected. Ok, I'll tell you, but it's going to cost you. What's the first childhood memory that pops into your head?"

He wondered if he should answer. O'Rourke had stopped kicking his chair. In for a penny in for a pound, so he answered, "When I was four, I remember blowing up an innertube until it popped. Interestingly, I have no memory of it actually popping, I just know that is what happened. I can remember the place. It was a pre-school that my mother worked at, but I seem to have blocked my reaction to the tube popping. It probably made me pee my pants. It's interesting how the mind blocks those memories it doesn't want you to retain." He thought about the last six months of his life and the memories he as trying to forget as well as those he wanted to retain forever. He knew he wasn't doing very well on either front. "Ok, your turn."

The smile had disappeared from her eyes. "Does the mind really block those memories that are too painful to hold on to? Or is that just bullshit?"

He was heading towards ground that he didn't want to cover. But still, he thought if he was going to gain anything, he needed to keeping moving forward. "It's been my experience that as memories age, they fade. Both the good and bad slowly leach from recollection and all you are left with is a shell. We try hard to remember the good, we keep mementos and tokens that help us retain what was enjoyable. But it all tends to fade to an outline of the actual event without constant reminding. And those reminders aren't always of the good times. People have all kinds of triggers that cause them to relive events that they would rather not. So, the answer to your question, at least from my perspective, is that the mind does what it can, but at the cost of things that you would really rather not lose. Nothing in life is free."

"You speak as if there has been considerable darkness in your life."

It was a question more than a statement. "My wife died in an automobile accident a year ago. But I don't want to say any more than that about it."

He tried to read her face; he knew that he would like this woman in different circumstances. Hell, he liked her now. Her head tilted to the side. Her eyes had lost the edginess they held earlier. Instead, she seemed to be playing memories through her mind. "My parents used to argue quite a bit. When they really got going, my sister and I would go outside to get away from the anger. The worst of the fights were usually at night, after my father had too much to drink. Outside, my sister would stare at the stars. She had names for some of them. She would tell me stories, mostly love stories, about them. She was convinced that the moon, named Luna of course, and the evening star, Venus, were frustrated lovers. She was about eight then, but wise beyond her years. I started calling her Celeste, as her mind was in the stars. It was a pet name that only I used. Those times, sitting outside with my sister staring at the stars, are some of my best memories even though they were often caused by things I would rather forget. But you're right. I know the spot we used to go to. I can still picture it clear in my mind even though I haven't been there in years. But the words we spoke, the feelings we shared, those are gone. But the bonds we built are strong. We might still fight from time to time, but I know that she will always be there for me if I need her. "

"Did she help you through Mark's father's death?"

"She did. Who's helping you through your wife's death?"

He couldn't tell her the whole truth and admit to her that her sister, PK, was. So, he responded with an answer that was true, just not complete. "My dog, Gunner, is leading the way. He loves me no matter what I do, and he knows just what to say when I need a lift."

"Your dog talks to you?"

"Not all communication is with speech. Sometimes a slobbery tongue can convey things much more clearly than the spoken word."

"Touché."

O'Rourke kicked his chair, or maybe she just bumped into it while changing position, but he kind of agreed that it was time to get back to work. "Tell me about Rickstraw?"

The anger returned to her eyes. But he didn't think it was directed at him. "Rickstraw was a memory that I would like to completely forget."

"Care to elaborate?" He also noticed that she has used the past tense. He wasn't sure if that was intentional or not.

There was another pause. He wondered if she was going to answer. He could see what appeared to be an internal struggle between continuing the conversation and keeping her mouth shut. "Rickstraw was an animal, and he took whatever he wanted."

Mark thought about the arrangement of the house and that Rickstraw didn't have a room. "Where did Rickstraw sleep?"

"Rickstraw slept wherever he wanted to."

"Did he sleep with you?"

She repeated, "He slept wherever he wanted to."

And so did Mark, "Did he sleep with you?"

"He slept wherever he wanted to."

He hadn't really expected this turn of events. "Did you have sex with him, was it consensual?"

She didn't answer verbally, but instead gave him a look that suggested *what the fuck do you think?*

"Tara, while your look clearly portrayed what happened, I need an answer."

"Yes, I had sex with him and no, it wasn't consensual."

"The kids?"

"No, he knew that if he ever touched my kids, I would kill him. Besides, that wasn't what he was about. He wanted to show that he could make you do whatever he wanted. He was on a power trip. It wasn't that he wanted sexual satisfaction from me. What turned him on was making me do whatever he wanted. It was all about power. Fucking pig!"

He knew that he was close to the line and probably had already strayed over it. She had provided a motive for Rickstraw's murder if he had in fact been killed. But he wanted to ask one more question. "You're a strong woman. What did Rickstraw have over you that would compel you to give in to his demands?"

"He had Sunny. I knew that he would kill him without a thought. As much as I despised what Sunny had become, a part of me still loved him. And my kids still thought the world of him. The risk wasn't worth the cost. So, I gave in. He never hit me or forced me. He knew that he didn't have to. And he rubbed it in Sunny's face. Sunny hated him."

"Did Sunny kill him?" The words came out before he had put any thought into what he was asking.

"Sunny isn't strong enough to do so something like that."

He knew it was time. Past time. "Tara, I have to read you your rights." He removed the card from his pocket and started to read. "You have the right to remain silent. Anything you say can and will be used against you in a court of law. You have the right to have an attorney present before and during questioning if you desire. If you cannot afford an attorney, one will be appointed to represent you free of charge. Do you understand these rights that I have explained to you?"

She looked at him but didn't answer. Her expression was more of *what the fuck* than anything else. This was why he hadn't wanted to go in this direction. But if he was going to keep asking her questions, there was a chance that she might say something that would incriminate herself. And he needed to have this step out of the way. "I need to get this out of the way, Tara. If you were to admit to anything and I didn't read your rights, some smart attorney would get your confession thrown out."

"I don't plan on confessing to anything," was her reply. "But yes, I understand my rights. And I am still willing to talk to you having those rights in mind."

"Sounds like you have heard somebody read from one of these cards before."

"I studied law for a while before I needed to move back home and help take care of my grandfather."

"Ok, that explains your knowledge of the Miranda Decision. I couldn't help but notice that when you mentioned Rickstraw, you spoke of him in the past tense. What makes you think that you won't have any new memories to try and repress?"

"I'm just confident that I won't ever see him again."

He thought for a second. "I borrowed Sunny's Cat and partially dug up what he spent the night trying to bury. It was Rickstraw's Jeep and it looked like there were two bullet holes in the windshield. You own guns. Did you shoot him?"

"I've never shot anyone, but if someone shot that asshole, I'd be happy to buy them a drink."

Mark paused briefly to confirm to himself that he wanted to challenge her now. He decided to issue a challenge, but not a harsh one. "You didn't shoot him. Sunny didn't shoot him. Yet, you're confident that he won't cause you anymore problems. How can you be so sure?"

Tara took in an exasperated breath. "We pride ourselves in being able to deal with our problems without help here." She waved her arm to show that she was referring the community that surrounded her home. "Rickstraw had done more than enough to attract the attention of some of the rougher neighbors. I received a message that he wouldn't be bothering me anymore. And I know my neighbors. He won't be bothering me anymore." She had a knowingly, sly smile on her face as she said this.

"Did you suborn Rickstraw's murder?" Mark asked.

"That's big word with only a few letters. No, I didn't ask anyone to kill him. I'm just glad that they did, if they did. If anyone deserved to be killed it was him."

"So, if you didn't ask someone to kill him, who told you that he was dead?"

She paused. He didn't think that she was going to answer. But she finally uttered, "My sister told me."

The pain in his gut returned with a vengeance. He was horrified by where this looked to be going. "So while you had a motive for wanting Rickstraw dead, appear to be somewhat gleeful at his apparent demise, and your husband spent the night burying the probable evidence, you want me to believe that your sister is responsible for his death?"

"I never said that my sister was responsible for his death. I only told you that she passed on a message to me."

"So how did she know he was dead if she wasn't involved?"

"I don't know, you'll have to ask her." Her eyes smiled as she said this. He wondered if PK had told her about him.

"Fair enough. Let me backtrack a bit. You mentioned that Rickstraw drew the attention of your neighbors." He used finger quotes when he said neighbors. "How did they know what was going on here. Did you tell them about Rickstraw?"

"I never told anyone about Rickstraw. It wasn't something that I was proud of."

"So, if you didn't tell them, who did?" Mark asked.

"I don't know that anyone told them. Rickstraw was throwing his weight around, trying to get something for nothing. He made threats."

"So, you think that Rickstraw was killed because he tried to extort your neighbors?"

"I think that was part of it."

"But not the only reason?"

"I don't know."

"If you didn't tell anyone what Rickstraw was doing, how did your neighbors know that he was raping you? Who knew what was going on? Did Sunny tell them?"

"Sunny was too much of a coward to protect his family and too proud to ask anyone for help. I don't know if the neighbors found out, but I am sure that Sunny didn't tell them. Maybe Rickstraw bragged about it, he was like that."

"So, who else knew that you were being forced to sleep with Rickstraw on a regular basis?" He was afraid to ask the question. Afraid to hear the answer. Afraid of what he might do afterwards.

"Celeste knew. I don't know how she knew, but she knew." And there it was.

"So, you think that your sister told someone that you were being raped and then that person killed him?" He paused before he added, "Did your sister kill him?" He couldn't believe that he had asked that question.

"I told you, I don't know who killed Rickstraw and if I did, I wouldn't tell you anyway."

"If Celeste told you that Rickstraw was dead, then she had to have known who killed him or done it herself." He realized that this was a statement and not a question. "Did your sister tell someone about Rickstraw and suggest that he be killed?" That may or may not be conspiracy to commit murder depending upon how you looked at it.

She didn't say a word. She just looked at him with those bright blue eyes and not a hint of emotion.

"Did Celeste ask someone to kill Rickstraw?" The question was just a whisper.

"I have told you more than I intended to, and I believe that I have fulfilled my obligation to society in trying to help you figure out who killed a man who was no friend to that same society. I'm done talking."

"What about your sister? Isn't she going to be angry that you threw her under the bus?" he asked even though she clearly had stated that she was done.

"Mr. Coltrane, you're a smart man. I don't think that my sister has anything to worry about, do you?"

She knew. She had set up a trap and he had fallen into it. She knew he wasn't going to help the detectives find "Celeste." And because she had appeared to cooperate, at least a little, it was unlikely that she was going to be going to jail today either.

As he got up, he looked at her and he could feel the smile form across his lips. "Tara Garvey, I think you're a pretty damn smart woman yourself."

Chapter Sixteen

Big Highway South of Small Town

December 24, 1996, 0236 Hours

It was a steady wall of water. His windshield wipers struggled to clear a path so he could see where he was going. Even at high speed, they couldn't keep up. He slowed further, crawling along at twenty-five miles per hour on the deserted freeway. It was about 2:30 in the morning and it had been raining all night. But not like this. He thought about parking and waiting out the deluge. Instead, he thought about the girl. He hadn't heard from her in more than a week, since the raid at her sister's house. He had called and left a couple of messages on her answering machine, but there had been no response. He didn't want to sound needy, and he didn't want to beg. He was beginning to think that the journey she had talked about was over. And he couldn't blame her. He and his cohorts had broken into her sister's house and dragged her out of bed at gunpoint. That would kill most relationships. Was this even a relationship? What was this? Pure lust? Or was there something more, something, beautiful?

It had been beautiful. The night in the rain, that would be a memory that he would hold and treasure for the rest of his life. He didn't want it to end, but at the same time, he was immensely grateful it had happened.

He saw the blinking yellow lights up ahead. His mind, reluctantly, returned to work. He slowed and came to a stop behind the Toyota Celica that was pulled to the side of the road with the hazard lights on. He turned on his rear flashers in the light-bar atop his patrol car. He noticed that the car in front of him was cock-eyed with the right-front wheel in the mud and the left rear wheel sticking across the fog line.

"Dispatch, A15, vehicle investigation," he spoke into the mike.

"A15, vehicle investigation," was the response. The dispatcher's tone suggested that she thought he was crazy.

"A15, vehicle investigation, northbound Big Highway, approaching Mill Town exit on a Toyota Celica, OnePaulQueenJohn246."

And the dispatcher parroted, "A15, vehicle investigation, northbound Big Highway approaching Mill Town on OnePaulQueenJohn246." She then added, "Vehicle is clear and current," letting him know that the car had not been reported stolen and that the registration was current.

He adjusted the towel that he had wrapped around his neck like a scarf. He had wrung it out after finishing his last call, a traffic accident on the freeway. A drunk driver had failed to negotiate the turn onto Four Mile Bridge and had hit the guardrail. Mark had stood the rain for more than an hour helping CHP to control traffic until the drunk's car could be removed, and the highway could be opened again. He added his rain-soaked ball cap to his attire and opened the door. A wall of water hit him as he got out. His supposedly waterproof jump suit was already stuck to his skin. He took his flashlight in his left hand and walked towards the car. Despite all the rain, the temperature was mild, and he was not at all cold. He thought it was kind of like taking a shower with your clothes on. It was another atmospheric river. He understood the concept better than most at this point in time.

He used his flashlight to illuminate the interior of the car as he approached on the passenger side. There was only one occupant, a young woman apparently asleep behind the wheel. She was wearing a raincoat over a green dress. He guessed that she was coming from a Christmas party. It was that time of year. As there were no other cars on the highway, he circled behind the car and came up to the driver's window. The woman was still oblivious to his presence despite the light. He knocked on the window. There was no response. He thought "oh shit" as he knocked harder. This time he saw her stir and he breathed a sigh of relief. But she still had not acknowledged him, so he knocked a third time. The woman startled and pulled away. Mark raised the flashlight so that she could see his uniform, but not so much that he couldn't still see inside of the car. She stopped recoiling, but still looked very uncomfortable about her current situation.

He knew that with the noise of the rain on the top of the car there was no way they could communicate through the closed window. He signaled for her to roll down the window by twirling his index finger. She wagged her head in a negative. He sighed and then used his "please don't make me use force" look. She didn't move. He reached for the door handle and found it unlocked. He pulled the door open. The smell of vomit and alcohol greeted him, despite the flood of rainwater between his nose and the car. He saw the remains of partially digested food on the inside of the door, although he guessed that the remains of her dinner wouldn't be there much longer as the rain blasted the door and the interior near it. The woman had crawled into the passenger seat, but he was ok with that for now. At least they could talk. He squatted down so that he could see into the car better. Her green dress had red stripes down the side, and there was a picture of Rudolph across her chest. Her hair was straight and shoulder length, framing an oval face. He thought she might be twenty-one, but probably younger.

"Are you ok?" he asked.

She nodded her head.

"Is your car running ok?"

Again, she nodded her head.

"Then why are you pulled to the side of the freeway in the worst rainstorm I can remember?"

She was silent for several seconds and then finally spoke for the first time, "I'm in trouble, aren't I?"

He answered her question with one of his own, "Why would you think you were in trouble?"

She looked down before raising her eyes and looking directly into his even though he doubted she could see them with his flashlight illuminating the inside of her car. "Because I was passed out drunk behind the wheel of my car might be one answer," she suggested.

He nodded his head. "Yes, if that was true, you could be in trouble. Is it?"

She didn't move, much less speak. They stared at each other in silence.

"A15, status check," came from his radio.

"A15 is code-four," was his response to his dispatcher.

The young woman asked, "What does that mean?"

"It means that I don't need any help, at least not right now. If I failed to answer, then they would send another car to check on me."

"So, it's just you and me? Do you really think you can handle me by yourself?" She had asked these two questions with a straight face and he wasn't sure if she was flirting or being aggressive.

Now it was his turn to be silent. He looked her in the face again. He tried to read her eyes, but there was no hint of what she was thinking there. But maybe that was it. She was thinking.

He finally uttered, "I don't think there is going to be anything to handle."

"Isn't that kind of cocky on your part?" she asked with just a hint of a smile.

"No, not at all. I don't think you're as drunk as you were, and I think you are smart enough not to do anything stupid."

Her smile broadened just a bit. "So, what do you suggest Officer Drowned Rat? How about closing my door before my car fills with water?"

"How about I give you a ride to somewhere you can spend the rest of the night and you come back and get your car in the daylight when the rain lets up? It can't keep raining like this for much longer. Where can I take you?"

She remained silent for several seconds. Her face was blank, but again he was pretty sure that she was thinking things through. He imagined her thoughts: It was dark, pouring rain, she was in the middle of nowhere without another person in sight, she was still a bit tipsy, and there was a man demanding that she go with him. Granted the man was a police officer, but did that really mean all that much in this day and age. "Is that my only option?" she finally asked.

"It's the only one that you are going to be happy with tomorrow." He wasn't sure that he had provided an answer that would convince her to override the normal concern she was feeling. But it was that or handcuffs and he didn't want to go there, not if he didn't have to.

171

"Why should I trust you?" she asked.

"I can't give you an answer that will make you feel more comfortable. The truth is that you don't have much choice. Either you come with me voluntarily or you get an early Christmas present of a new pair of shiny bracelets. There is a lesson to be learned here about planning and knowing your limitations. But you can gain this wisdom with some mild angst or with a free night's lodging that is guaranteed to ruin your holiday spirit. The choice is yours."

"Angst, who talks like that?" was her only response.

"I read a lot."

She smiled just a little bit. It was a nice smile. "You're not real convincing, but you are honest. My parents live in River City. I'll accept your offer of a ride. What now?"

"Stay here, I have to rearrange my front seat so there's room for you."

He returned to his car, moved his patrol bag and a couple of empty Diet Coke cans to the back seat. When he returned to the Celica, he carried an umbrella in addition to his flashlight. He opened the Celica's passenger door while holding the umbrella overhead. The woman stepped out. He handed her the umbrella and asked her to wait by his car while he did a better job of parking hers. She slowly moved towards the lights of his vehicle. He moved the driver's seat back and climbed behind the wheel. The car was similar to a car his wife had owned when they were married, same model, just a different color. His mind tumbled.

He felt the blackness return. He turned the key. The motor started and Garth Brooks' voice boomed from the speakers:

I could have missed the pain
But I'd of had to miss the dance.

Shit, that was the last thing he needed to hear right now. He mashed the stereo power button with his index finger. He sat still for a couple of seconds, feeling the wave of depression flow over him. Karen's image flowed through his mind. But he crawled through to the surface and took a breath. This was not the time, nor was it the place. He knew he would pay for this later, but he was working, and he couldn't break down now. He put the car into reverse to ease it out of the mud and then straightened it out so that it was close to the edge of the asphalt and completely on the shoulder.

As he walked back to his car, he could feel the warm tears flowing down his cheeks, the hint of salt on his lips. He knew that he couldn't just shut off his emotions. He stopped, took off his hat, and raised his head towards the clouds. He could feel the rain pound against his flesh, taking his tears away in a relieving flood. He thanked Mother Nature for her gifts, and then returned to the present. The young woman was watching him as he approached.

"Are you alright? I thought maybe you were trying to drown yourself."

He raised his flashlight and saw that she was smiling, but it was a smile of curiosity mixed with just a hint of concern. He opened his passenger door for her. "It's a long story that I don't really want to talk about."

"I'm a good listener and I like stories," was her response, said with an open smile that he couldn't see but could feel in her tone.

He didn't say anything as she made herself comfortable in his front seat. But as he settled behind the wheel, he told her, "I'm sorry, but it wouldn't be professional to tell you my tale of woe. Maybe another time, in another place. But thank you for your concern."

"Dispatch, A15 is 10-14 with an X-ray to River City. Break for mileage"

"Roger, A15 is 10-14 with an X-ray, go ahead with mileage."

"A15, mileage is 38.6."

"A15 is 10-14 with an X-ray to River City, starting mileage is 38.6, time is 0248 hours."

This time she didn't ask him about the radio traffic. They headed north in silence, his speed slow. He could tell that she was watching him; could feel her eyes on his face. But he didn't speak. Instead, she broke the silence. "I've had a few dealings with law enforcement before, maybe more than a few. The cops have always come across as hard and impermeable. They're only concerned with calming the waters enough that they can move on to the next trouble spot. And if that means taking someone to jail, that's a bonus. It's nice to see that at least some of you are human, that you can feel emotions, that you have some empathy. It's comforting to know that you're not an automaton. That's what makes me feel safe."

A smile started to form on his face. Without thinking, he uttered, "Thanks for noticing." It was the same phrase that PK used every time that he told her she was beautiful. As soon as the words found life, her image came to him and he could feel her body against his, the rain beating down upon them both. His smile turned to a shit-eating grin.

"Something just happened. Are you ok? Having some kind of bipolar event?" she asked with a voice that contained a bit humor and just a bit of concern once again.

"No, I'm fine. 'Thanks for noticing' is a phrase that a friend of mine uses. She's been helping me through a tough time." His tone was upbeat.

"Girlfriend?" she asked.

"It's complicated."

"That's not an answer. Are you sleeping with her?"

"Hey, I'm the one that's supposed to ask all the questions."

"So, are you?"

"Am I what?"

"Sleeping with her?"

He thought briefly about just staying quiet, but he liked this woman, liked the way she thought. "We've slept together, but we haven't had sex, at least not yet…. and maybe not ever."

"Do you want to?"

"Do I want to what?"

"Do you want to have sex with her?"

This caused him to pause. It was his turn to think. Is that what he wanted? There was a part of him, mainly between his legs, that thought that was a great idea. But he realized that he valued her companionship, the warmth that she brought him, more than the release that would come from sex. And he was afraid that a sexual act would be the end of the journey. That is, if it wasn't already over.

"I'm a man, so it would be dishonest of me to say no. But it's not as simple as pure lust. She provides a companionship that I crave and that may be as powerful as the desire I feel," was the answer that eventually slipped through his lips. "It's the feel of her next to me that I want, I think more than the feeling of ecstasy."

"Oooh, this is complicated. What are you afraid of? Love? Commitment? Or maybe it's that you don't think your relationship will support both sex and companionship?"

"Who are you?" he asked?

"I read a lot," was her answer.

"Bullshit!"

"I'm a marriage and couples' counselor."

"You don't look old enough to have graduated high school, much less to have a master's degree."

"I'm twenty-three. I do read a lot and I'm pretty smart. I graduated from Sacramento State at twenty, and finished my masters at the University last year. I started working with one of my professors there, counseling couples. I am also part of a team that tries to work with those in mental crisis, often in the company of, but not assisted by law enforcement." There was a slight pause and then she added, "What I don't do very much is drink."

There was silence in the car for several miles. He had always been comfortable in silence, but not now for some reason. "You're more right than I think you know. I don't think my relationship, if I even have one still, will survive, sex or not. There are just too many external factors."

"External factors? What does that mean?"

"It's kind of like the Montagues and Capulets."

"Romeo and Juliet? Is there a blood feud between your families? Did you kill her cousin? But more importantly, are you considering suicide if this doesn't work out?" The last was said with a bit jest, but just a bit.

Mark laughed for a moment, before tyring to recall the last time he had done so. "You do read, and you have a good memory. No, it's not quite that bad. But her family has no love for my profession, I arrested her brother-in-law, and I helped serve a search warrant at her sister's house that dragged the sister out of bed at gunpoint."

Now it was her turn to laugh. She was silent for a while and then she asked in a quiet, but sympathetic tone, "What's the real problem? There's something lying underneath this thing you have that makes the relationship important, but that also makes it difficult. You were crying in the rain; something had to cause that and I'm pretty sure it wasn't this woman. You beamed when you thought of her. Do you suffer from PTSD, grief, or some other mental trauma?"

He wondered if he should be annoyed. This woman was delving into parts of his psyche that he was not even sure that he understood. But he had also found that talking about his grief, especially with someone who understood, might make him cry and feel like shit in the short term, but was beneficial in the long run. It helped him to process what had happened to him and maybe where he was going in the future. This woman asked the right questions; she could read him more accurately than anyone he spoken to yet. So, he figured he might as well make use of the opportunity.

"My wife died in an automobile accident a year ago, right before Christmas. She used to drive a car like yours, same year and model, but a different color. She traded it for the car she died in. When I got inside of your car, it was a trigger, and I couldn't hold my grief back. You weren't supposed to see my tears. The rain was supposed to wash them away." And then after a short pause, "If only it was that easy."

She took her time processing his words, the sentiment that was carried in the lilt of his voice. As they neared River City, she spoke. Her voice was soft, her cadence was slow; it was apparent that considerable thought had gone into her words. "I know enough to know that I have only a little idea what you are going through. I have read about grief, understand what causes it, the stages you process through. But I know that this is just the basic foundation of understanding your turmoil. I don't have the experience to help you deal with the loneliness, the loss of the most important person in your life. I know I can't imagine this. So, my ability to provide worthwhile suggestions is pretty limited. I have a mentor; a wonderful woman who has experienced much of what life has to offer, including grief on multiple levels. She lives in Weedtown and probably knows your girl's family; she knows everyone there. One of her favorite offerings is that if it feels good, do it; if it stops feeling good, then stop. In my experience, it sounds much simpler than it is. I would add only that you should enjoy the moment, but when it is gone, let it go. Retain the memories but use them to give you the strength to move on and don't get caught in trying to go back. The past is behind us and we need to look forward. Does that make sense?"

She paused for just a bit and then added, "And sex— sex is a great healer in and of itself. I hear what you are saying. I can't comprehend your fear as I don't understand its basis. But I would encourage you, if the situation presents itself, to share what your friend is willing to offer. You said that you crave the feel of her next to you. That I can understand. Almost all of us crave the feeling of being wanted, of being needed, of being loved. Don't be afraid to share what you have to offer." She put heavy emphasis on the word *you* "It may be what your girl is looking for. After all, if nothing is risked, nothing is gained."

Her words rolled through his mind as he took the River City exit from the freeway. The rain had finally let up and the beat provided by the windshield wipers slowed. As he stopped in front of the address she had provided, he told her, "You are wise beyond your years. Thank you for helping me put things in perspective. I will think about what you have told me, but I do believe that you have chosen the right career. You are extremely perceptive for one so young."

The lights in the house were on and he saw the door open. A man of about fifty years of age came out and stood on the porch. He was dressed in pajamas and he looked at the patrol car parked in front of his house with significant trepidation.

"Your father?" he asked. When she nodded, he added "You should go before he gets more worried. But thank you for your help. It was unexpected, but timely."

She reached across the radios and control boxes that separated the seats and kissed his cheek. "Thank you, Officer Coltrane for the ride home. My name, by the way, is Pam. You never asked."

She opened the car door and ran through the mist to her father who still waited on the porch. Her father wrapped his arms around her and led her into the house. Mark smiled.

"A15 is clear. Ending mileage is 48.2."

"Roger, A15 is clear, ending mileage is 48.2 at 0314 hours."

Chapter Seventeen

Small Town

December 24, 1996, 0455 Hours

He drove around Small Town in the dark; the wipers still belting out a slow and steady beat. He parked above the river and watched as it flowed by his vantage point. He thought it was likely to flood with the amount of rain they had been receiving. If so, they would have to move the trailers out of the park, but that was for another day and, hopefully, a different shift. Now he thought about PK and what Pam had said. 'Retain the memories but use them to move forward.' When he thought of PK, he felt warm and comforted. When he thought of Karen, he felt lost and alone. One was a possibility, the other was dead and gone. Why did he dwell on the past and his losses when it was time to move forward? Was that what Pam was telling him? If only it was that simple. But he had good memories of Karen too. Was that what Pam was saying? When the blackness hit, try and focus on the good times and use that to move forward. But that was a duel-edged sword, he had found; trying to focus on the memories he treasured most made him miss her even more. *Shit!* This wasn't getting him anywhere. It was time to drive around and see if there was someone he could roust to get his mind clear.

He couldn't find anyone to talk to. Even the bad guys were smart enough to get out of the rain. He headed back to the station and was surprised to see the chief's car parked in the lot. It was 5:30 in the morning. What was he doing here? He walked in the back door and found the chief in his office.

"Good morning Chief. What brings you here on such a glorious morning?"

"I couldn't sleep. I thought I would come in so that you could take off a bit early. It's Christmas Eve. I'm sure you have things to do."

Mark was a bit surprised by this response. The old chief never covered any part of a shift for him, much less on Christmas Eve. He was beginning to like this man.

The chief could see the confusion on his face and added, "I've already celebrated with my wife and she is headed off to be with her family tomorrow. Why don't you take off tonight about an hour after the bars close and put me on call? That way you can spend some quality time in the morning with your family and friends."

Mark knew that the chief and his wife had separated, but he had not realized that meant that he would be alone on Christmas. "Thank you Chief, that's very generous. But I don't have any family here either and my roommates have all gone home for the holidays."

"Then get some extra sleep and consider it a present from me. And by the way, here's another present. It came in the mail yesterday."

The chief handed him a box wrapped in brown paper. It was addressed to him at the Small Town Police Department. It had some heft. He looked closer at the label; the return address was 123 Main Street in Anytown, USA. He was a bit surprised that the post office would deliver such a thing. When he looked at the postmark, however, he noticed that the package had been mailed in Weedtown. After his recent experiences, he had learned that things were a bit different down there and maybe that included the local post office.

He turned the package over. He saw that where the paper that bound the box was taped to itself, there were two, little, watercolor paintings. One was of a crescent moon. The other was a star. *Venus and Luna,* he thought to himself, *frustrated lovers.*

His Chief asked in half-jest, "Should I call the bomb squad?"

"No, Chief, I think I know who sent me this, but I don't have any idea what's inside."

"Does this friend of yours want to kill you?"

"I don't think so, at least not yet," was the only answer that he could think of.

The Chief looked at the same paintings he had seen. "Is it from a woman?"

"Yeah, I think it is from Tara Garvey, Sunshine Garvey's wife. I interviewed her during the warrant service."

"Well, take it in the squad room to open, I'm too young to die if you're wrong," the Cheif said, then he went back into his office and closed the door.

Mark took the box from the front counter and carried it to the table in the squad room. He used the small blade on his Swiss army knife to cut the tape. As he removed the brown paper wrapper, he discovered a Redwing boot box that was also taped shut. His knife made short work of the remaining tape and he opened the box with an apprehension that took him by surprise.

Nothing blew up. Instead, he found a 3X5 card that simply read:

I thought you could use these more than I could. Merry Christmas.

He pulled aside some wadded up newspaper and found two items. The first was a gallon size Ziploc bag that held what looked to be about a pound of meth. He belatedly found some latex gloves and put them on. He removed the bag and underneath was a Kimber, stainless steel, .45 caliber pistol with wood grips. The gun, with the slide locked back, was attached to a piece of cardboard with zip-ties. A longer zip-tie ran through the magazine well and the opening in the slide, keeping the action from closing. A loaded magazine was also zip-tied to the same piece of cardboard. And a small, coin-sized Ziploc that had been stapled to the cardboard held a single .45 cartridge. The cardboard and all of its attachments were also sealed in a large Ziploc bag. He put the meth back in the box and reached for the phone.

He called Mulhouse at the Task Force Office and was a bit surprised to actually find him there. He told Mulhouse what he had been sent in the mail and Mulhouse agreed to come take the evidence from him. As he finished the call, his Chief came out of the office.

"I didn't hear anything go boom, so I figured it was safe to come out now." His Chief was smiling as he said this. Mark was not sure just how to read this man yet. Was he making fun of him? He didn't know, but he decided that he had better show him what was in the box. The Chief looked at the dope and the gun. "Well, it appears you were right. She wasn't trying to kill you. But she sure is adding to your reputation as a shit-magnet. Can you trace the package back to her?"

"Given what I have learned about SoCo, I doubt the Post Office would be willing to help at all. I can try if you like, though."

"Don't bother." He paused briefly and then added, "That's several thousand dollars' worth of meth and a thousand-dollar pistol. She could have sold both in Soco very easily. Interesting woman. Did you leave a message with the Task Force?"

"Mulhouse was actually there; I have no idea why this early in the morning. But he's going to come down and pick up both items as they are linked to his case more than anything we have going on here."

"Cool beans!" the Cheif responded. "Put evidence tags on them and then take off. I'll hold down the fort." Then he returned to his office, leaving the door open this time.

Mark took the items to the evidence counter and filled out the tags. He placed the handgun, still in the original Ziploc, into a cardboard box and sealed it with evidence tape. He then wrote his initials and the date so that the letters covered both the tape and the box. The Ziploc of meth went into a large manila envelope which was also sealed with tape, dated, and initialed. Mulhouse probably would have wanted to see them first, but now he could only do so if he broke the seals. Not a big deal, but it would probably piss him off regardless. He took the box and the bag and left them underneath the front counter in the outgoing box. He started to strip off his gear in preparation for heading home when the phone rang. Before he could reach the nearest extension, he heard the chief pick it up.

"Coltrane, the phones for you. She wouldn't tell me her name but said that it was a personal call." The chief smiled broadly as he stepped out of the office to address him. "Are you still seeing that hippie girl?"

Mark picked up the phone next to where he was standing and moved so that he could see the chief hang up his headset. Only then did he take the phone off of hold and speak.

"This is Officer Coltrane."

"We need to talk."

He recognized PK's voice and butterflies started to fly through his belly. "Yes, we do."

"What time do you get off work?"

"The chief said I can leave anytime."

"Meet me for breakfast at the café in Wide Spot in the Road?"

"I can do that, but I don't have much in the way of clothes to change into. I'll look kind of like a cop."

"Do the best you can. They open at 6:00. I'll be there waiting for you." As Mark hung up the phone, he couldn't tell if she was mad, rushed, or just being abrupt. He headed to his locker and took off his uniform shirt and Kevlar vest, hanging them next his gun belt. His white T-shirt would have to do. He put on his black raincoat, bid the chief goodbye, and headed to his car.

Chapter Eighteen

Café on the Old Highway

December 24, 1996, 0605 Hours

He raced down the narrow two-lane highway. The rain was only a gentle mist now and wisps of river fog lay in the trees. He pushed his car as fast as he dared, slowed only by the wet asphalt and the leaf litter on the highway. He was not sure why. Did he need to get there before she tired of waiting for him and left? He realized that his heart was pounding. Was it the drive? Or was it that he was so unsure of what this meeting would bring? Perhaps a bit of both? He elected to slow down just a bit. He wouldn't do himself any good if he wrapped his car around an old-growth redwood. Would it be ironic that he killed himself the same way that Karen had? Maybe, but Karen was playing stupid car tricks with a friend, while he was trying to meet a woman that he cared for. Were the motivations that much different? Maybe, maybe not. He slowed down some more, bringing the speedometer down to about 60 as he eased through a gentle S curve. And then PK's image came to his mind, brilliant blue eyes sparkling, and he slowed some more. He heard her say "enjoy the journey." He downshifted and looked around. Even in the dark, this was still the most beautiful road he had ever seen. Maybe he shouldn't treat it like a racecourse. His eyes tried to take in more than the dashed yellow line in front of him. Occasionally, he could see the river flowing near flood stage to his right. His high beams picked out mist floating in the canyons on the far side of the river. Trees, most eight to ten feet in diameter, marched right up to the edge of the roadway. He took a deep breath. Whatever was going to happen, would happen. Don't fuck it up by overthinking.

When he pulled into Wide Spot in the Road, the only vehicle he could see was PK's Toyota parked in front of the Café. He parked in the adjacent perpendicular parking spot. He stretched, hands reaching towards the cloud covered sky, as he got out of his low-slung car. It had been a long night and it was catching up with him. He noticed that the sign in the window said that the Café was closed, but the door was unlocked. As he entered the restaurant, it was déjà vu all over again. He wasn't sure whose line that was, but he kind of liked it. PK was the only person in the restaurant. She sat at the same table as before, wore the same hat, the same sweater. He plopped down in the chair across from her, all semblance of grace having been abandoned.

PK held her coffee cup in front of her face as she sipped her morning stimulant. He thought he could see the corners of her lips turn up in a half smile, but he was not sure. Her eyes, however, bore him into as if trying to bypass his face and going straight for his mind. That didn't worry him too much this morning. He was so tired that his mind was like the night sky, nothing but clouds and fog. He returned her gaze and saw the specks of color in her irises that so intrigued him. He couldn't help but smile.

He heard, "You look beautiful this morning," utter from his lips without realizing the conscious thought of saying it.

She lowered the coffee mug and sat it on the table. "Thank you for noticing," was all she said in response. He still couldn't read her even as her eyes bore into him and the hint of a smile rested on her lips. He couldn't figure out if it was the look of a cat about to play with her prey, or if she was happy to see him. Then he realized that perhaps it was both. A quick image of Tara with the same look passed quickly through his mind. They were definitely sisters. But that was about as much thought as he could muster. He figured that he would put it into words, what the hell.

"I feel like a beat-up mouse being stared at by a cat just before she bites my head off."

The corners of her lips turned up just a hint, but the eyes didn't change. She still didn't utter a word.

"Are you just going to play with me before you give me the coup de grâce?"

And that did it. Her face broke into a grin and her eyes sparkled with affection. "I couldn't do it; I couldn't be angry with you. There's something about you, Officer Coltrane, that has found a way inside of me, to a place I guard tightly." She raised the mug to her lips and continued to watch him, waiting for him to make the next move.

Fortunately, he was saved by the cook, who placed a glass of what looked like Diet Coke in front of him along with a warmer full of fresh tortillas. He departed but returned almost immediately with a huge plate that held at least a half-dozen eggs that had been scrambled with chorizo. In addition, there were large portions of rice and beans. This was followed by smaller plates, napkins, and eating utensils. And then the cook was gone, leaving him alone once more to face the enigma that sat across from him.

But when his gaze returned to the woman before him, her manner had changed once again. She was ladling food onto her plate. Without looking at him, she asked, "Did you know it was my sister's scene before you got there?"

"No, I wouldn't have gone if I had known. But I wouldn't have told you they were coming either."

"Fair enough. When did you figure it out?"

"You and your sister have a strong familial resemblance, especially in your eyes. I wondered briefly when I first saw her, but I didn't want to believe it. So, I didn't. It wasn't until I went into her room and saw your family picture that I had to accept the situation."

"You were looking at her eyes, were you?" She tilted her head to the side as she asked the question and he once more felt like he was looking at the Cheshire cat.

"I was trying to," he answered, mostly honestly. "But she does have a lovely figure for a woman who has borne two children."

"You men are all alike. You see a couple of boobs and all rational thought goes out the window." She was smiling as she said this, however. "She likes you by the way, my sister that is. She didn't realize who you were until you started to pay attention to her children. At first, she thought of you as just another pig, but when you had Svetlana pick a movie and Mark start a fire, she started to pay attention. It was when you brought them cereal that she saw the patches on your uniform and then she looked at the name on your chest. Up 'til then, she just wanted to see you as another human animal who had come to prey on her family and their way of life. But then she realized how close-minded she was being and started to put two and two together. She enjoyed playing mind games with you; she likes to do that. She wanted to make you squirm just a bit; payback if you will. But she realized afterwards that she may have gone too far."

"I was squirming alright, but what made her think that she went too far?"

"Because that cute little girl you had with you figured out what was going on. Tara is pretty sure that she realized that you knew who "Celeste" was. The detective's attention changed from her to you during that part of the interrogation. You couldn't see it because she was behind you. Tara wasn't trying to get you into trouble, just screw with you a bit."

"I'm not in any trouble that I am aware of," was his guarded response.

"Would you get into trouble if you knew who I was and didn't tell them?"

"If Detective O'Rourke learns that we are close, then I would be consorting with a possible suspect in a murder investigation and I might lose my job. It wouldn't be too bad if I stopped seeing you, but if I continue, it shows my lack of judgment. But I'm not aware that she is pushing the issue at all. I haven't heard a thing from my new chief. In fact, he's been treating me really well lately."

"Are you going to tell them about me?"

He paused briefly to get the right words together, "No, I'm not. I care too much about you to put you in the center of their investigation. But at the same time, if I am asked questions, I need to answer them. I can't lie for you."

Her eyelids closed for just a second and then those amazing orbs returned to the light once again. Her face did not show much emotion, but her eyes beckoned him in. "Do you want to know my role in Rickstraw's demise?"

He couldn't read her. His mind was still fogged despite the adrenalin that was coursing through his body from her presence. He knew this was a loaded question. If she told him, it might be more than he could hold back from O'Rourke. If he didn't know, the question would fester in his soul for as long as he as he was close to this woman. But did this thing, this journey that they shared, did they have that much more road to travel. His brain was starting to hurt.

"Your hesitation is understandable. Let me make it easier for you. I'm leaving for Ecuador the day after tomorrow. If your girlfriend, the detective, finds us together, you're likely to lose your job. I don't know a lot about men, but I do understand that your role as a police officer is a core part of the way you see yourself. If you lost that, you would have to reinvent yourself and you would resent what I did to you for the rest of your life. I care too much about you to do that. I had an opportunity to join a team studying agroforestry in the rainforests and I took it. I will be out of the country for a year or more. In that time, you will find another woman and your need for me will wane. You may even forget about me." This last came with a wink and grin that made it clear that she didn't think that was the case. "And maybe Detective O'Rourke will grow tired of looking for me. She has been, you know. She stopped at both my aunt's and my parent's houses asking about me. She got nothing of course, but she doesn't appear to be giving up easily."

He sat there stunned. He had thought this might be coming to an end, but not this way. Before he could speak, however, she continued, "I want you to know that I don't feel any remorse. Rickstraw was an animal and he got less than he deserved. If you don't want to know, I won't say any more."

"Ecuador? You're going to Ecuador?" He was not thinking about Rickstraw, or murder, or his career; he was thinking about the stunningly beautiful woman sitting across the table from him.

She watched him in silence for what seemed like forever but was only a few seconds. "I surprised you with that, didn't I?" When he nodded his agreement, she continued, "It's for the best. You won't have to worry about how my actions may affect you in the future and I won't be around for your girlfriend to find."

"You keep calling her my girlfriend, but she's not, you are." The words were out of his mouth before his brain processed what he was saying.

Now it was her turn to reflect on what was being said. "Do you consider me your girlfriend? That suggests some permanency and exclusiveness. I offered you neither and was pretty up-front about it. Is this going to be a problem?"

"No, I'm tired and that's not the right word. I am not sure what the word is to describe our relationship to each other. The connection is pretty nebulous, but there is a connection. I can feel it here." He tapped his chest above his heart as he said this. "But you are correct, you never promised me more than your company. I think I always knew that this wouldn't last, but because I didn't want it to end, I didn't think about it. That includes how we were going to say good-bye. I never would have dreamed that you would invite me to breakfast and then tell me that you were going to South America." He began to smile, faint at first, but then it grew to encompass most of his face, but not his eyes. "When do you leave?"

"My plane leaves from San Francisco the day after tomorrow. Why are you suddenly smiling? Are you happy I'm leaving?" This last tidbit was said with a smile and wink.

"Sometimes it is easier to smile than it is to cry. I was thinking that all you promised me was a journey. And I must say that it has been a hell of a trip. I just didn't expect it to end at a breakfast table."

He watched as the corners of her mouth widened just a bit and the sparkle returned to her eyes. She whispered, "It's not over yet, Officer Coltrane."

Now, he tilted his head to the side and looked at her with a question mark all over his face, but he didn't say a word. He had found that sometimes the best way to get information was not to ask any questions and let the other person fill the silence.

They stared at each other, each looking the other in the eyes. He knew he could get lost in there. Perhaps a bit surprisingly, they both felt comfortable in the silence as if it was meant to be and they didn't need words to communicate how they felt. He could hear rain start to fall heavily on the building's metal roof, but still he focused on her face, on the tiny wrinkles around her eyes, the flare of her nose, and the curve of her lips. This was the most beautiful woman he had ever sat across a table from. It wasn't just the contours of her face, but it was the way she looked at him that made her so attractive.

She finally broke the silence, "Enough gaga eyes. Tomorrow is Christmas, but I don't have to be at my parent's house until about noon. We're going to have an early dinner and open some more presents. Then they are going to drive me to the airport the next day. But I have the morning free until about 10:00. What time do you get off of work, Officer Coltrane?"

Before he could think about what she was saying, he uttered, "The chief told me I could go home an hour after the bar closes. Last year they closed at midnight, but it could be sooner or later depending on how busy they are."

Peacekeepers

"I have a gift for you that still needs some work. Come to the cabin when you can. I'll be there. Don't worry about the time. I'll either be awake or sleeping very lightly. And bring some of your favorite music, a disc or two." As the realization of what she was saying spread across his face, she added, "The journey's not over, not yet sweetheart."

She stood. "Armando is an old friend of mine. We went through school together. He taught me all the dirty words in Spanish. He knows of you too. His sister, Elena, lives in Small Town. I think you know her. I asked him to make us breakfast as a favor to me and he agreed. Don't try and pay him or leave him a tip, it will only offend him. I'll see you in the wee hours of the morning."

She planted a sloppy kiss on his cheek and walked out the door. There seemed to be just a hint more sway in her hips as she departed. His mind was still fogged and rather than think about what had just been said, he looked at the food before him. They had both been so busy talking and engrossed in each other that they had hardly made more than a small dent in the plate's contents. But it smelled fantastic even if it was not real hot anymore. His stomach growled as he reached for the serving spoon.

Chapter Nineteen

College Town

December 24, 1996, 1328 Hours

He had tossed and turned in bed all day. Gunner had tried his best to provide the comfort he needed, but his mind refused to shut down. Even a second shower had not helped him to relax to the point of sound sleep. His mind turned over what PK had told him at breakfast. She was leaving the country. She hadn't denied any involvement in Rickstraw's apparent killing either, and she wanted him to come to her cabin tonight. He wanted to know what she knew, but then again, he didn't. He could not fathom that this beautiful young woman was part of something so insidious as murder. She might even have pulled the trigger. But the more he thought about that possibility, he knew it wasn't true. PK might be a lot of things, but a cold-blooded killer wasn't one of them.

And then his mind shifted gears from the past to the future. He tried to formalize what he would say to her tonight at her cabin. Should he say anything? Should he even go? Was ignorance truly bliss? As these questions rolled through his head, his mind again switched gears, back to the past and the look in her eyes as they had stood in the rain. His mind stopped tumbling as he felt the heat of her body against his once again. He relaxed, his breathing slowed, and he dreamed of blonde hair, blue eyes, and cat claws. Gunner felt his human relax as he lay curled up next to his abdomen. He emitted a sigh, wondering what troubled his man. Humans could be so difficult, but now confident that this moment's crisis had passed, he too, started to dream.

The two, man and dog, passed the afternoon together in sound slumbers, each dreaming of things close, but just out of reach. Both creatures' subconscious minds dealt with lust; one sexual, the other blood, as Gunner raced across endless fields trying without success to catch that elusive quail. But both awoke to the sound of the phone ringing. Mark reluctantly reached for the receiver next to his bed and managed to remove it from the cradle before the answering machine clicked on.

"Hello."

"I'm sorry, I didn't mean to wake you. I thought you would be up by now." His groggy mind didn't recognize the female caller's voice. It was familiar, but he couldn't place it.

Before his thoughts clicked into place, he responded, "I had a rough morning and didn't sleep well."

He heard the soft chuckle followed by, "I bet." His mind was beginning to clear, and he realized he needed to be more careful about what he said.

His suspicions were confirmed when the caller added, "I'll let you go back to sleep. I'll catch you when your shift starts tonight."

The caller's voice was that of Detective O'Rourke. "Shit." He wasn't sure if he had said the word out loud or it had just silently passed through his thoughts.

"Why don't you come early so I can handle my calls if there are any pending. I'll be there by 1800."

"Ok Mark. I'm sorry I woke you. I'll see you in a couple of hours." He heard the click of the receiver on the other end of the line.

Gunner looked at him, his brown eyes showing worry, his head cocked to the side in a question mark. Had he learned that body language from his dog? Maybe. He reached over and scratched the dog's head. "Don't worry boy, things will be ok." He threw back the covers and began to prepare for a new day, one that would ask questions, and maybe, just maybe, answer a few as well.

He didn't have anything else to do; his last-minute Christmas shopping was done, and he didn't have time to do any real baking. Besides, who would he be baking for? The guys at the department? They could make their own cookies. So, he got dressed and headed to work. The roads were crowded with families headed to visit their loved ones. He couldn't help but compare his evening to theirs, but he kind of liked working Christmas Eve. People were in such good moods, and it was easy to chat with just about everyone. And since he didn't have children or family close by, while the other officers did, beside the Chief, it only seemed fair that he sacrifice just a bit. It was Christmas Day that he didn't like working. About mid-afternoon, multiple families had consumed too much alcohol and the goodwill towards others had been worn down by underlying animosity. He believed that Christmas was a holiday to celebrate with those you loved, and it was an opportunity to show your generosity to your loved ones, as well as everyone else worldwide. It was a time to feel joy, to realize how much good there was in the world. The family 415s, arguments, and even fistfights on this day reinforced his cynicism and made him question some of his long-held beliefs that people were inherently good. It didn't help that he had met some truly bad people. But he refused to let the flashing image of Rickstraw's picture bring him down. He felt good. He wasn't sure why. Perhaps it was the holiday spirit, perhaps it was the thought that something he dreaded would soon be over, and perhaps, just perhaps, it was the thought that he would be seeing PK once again before the night was over.

He arrived at the station and was a little surprised to notice that the chief's car was still there. He walked in the back door and found the chief behind his desk. No one else was around. His good mood was beginning to fade just a bit as he realized that it would not be long before he was the one being interrogated. And the chief would want to know what was going on when O'Rourke arrived. He knew he should tell him. With some trepidation, he walked to the door of his office. The chief was peering at this computer screen, but Mark was fairly sure the chief knew he was standing there.

"Boss, you got some time?"

The older man looked up and took him in. "I'm just checking some research on stocks. I can give you as much time as you need unless a crisis occurs out there on the mean streets." The chief looked him over once again. "You look like you are about to confess to a murder. You're not going to do that are you? I need someone to cover town tonight." This last statement was said with a rather large grin.

"How much do you know about Rickstraw's death?"

"I've read your reports and I have heard a bit through the rumor mill. What do you think I should know?"

Mark realized that the chief was giving him room to hang himself, but also to phrase the conversation how he wanted it to go. "Did you know that Tara Garvey and my girlfriend are sisters?"

The chief smiled, "That must have been a bit awkward."

Mark was tuned in enough to realize that the chief had not answered his question. He guessed that meant that the chief knew some of his problem, maybe most of it. He might as well tell him the whole story. And so he did.

As Mark spoke, he watched the chief. He could tell the other man was listening, both with his ears and his eyes. He didn't interrupt with questions, but rather, let Mark tell the story from beginning to end. But there was no betrayal of what the man was thinking. Nor could he tell how much, if any, of this information was new to his boss. When he was finished, including that Detective O'Rourke would be here shortly to talk to him, he waited for his boss to chew him out for making bad choices and not being more forthright. That's what the old boss would have done.

But instead, the chief answered, "That's a good story. You should write a book about it. And by the way, it was some really good police work. You should be proud of yourself. I know I am."

Mark was stunned into silence. This was not what he had expected. Not at all.

The silence filled the room. It seemed like minutes, but it was probably only a handful of seconds before the chief asked in a quiet, but more serious tone, "What's the problem?"

Mark didn't know how to answer. It was obvious that the chief had listened to him. Couldn't he see what his problem was? But before he could try and frame an answer the chief spoke again, "Let me rephrase that: what do you think the problem is?"

"I'm in love with a girl who is involved in a murder."

"You love her?" the chief asked with a large smile, but before Mark could answer, the chief asked another question, "Do you think that she pulled the trigger?"

"There's a lot about her I don't know, but I am confident that she is not a killer, not like this, anyway. In the heat of the moment, I don't know, does anyone really know what another person will do when their life or a loved one's is at stake. But she wouldn't kill from ambush, of that I'm sure."

"But you think that there's a chance that she might have told someone else what was happening to her sister, knowing that person would take action?"

Mark smiled sadly, "I think that's a distinct possibility."

"And you think some smart detective is going to think that is the same as soliciting murder and will arrest her?"

Mark only nodded his head in response.

"You know that would never be prosecuted? There's no way an attorney could prove her intent beyond a reasonable doubt."

Mark's smile stayed on his face as his heart dropped into his abdomen. "I understand that, but it's irrelevant. I would know. I don't think I could love someone, no matter their reasoning, who would try to arrange another's murder."

"I've never met your girl. I know only what I have been told about her. But I have watched you for the last couple of months. That girl was exactly what you needed. She showed you that life was worth living again. Before, you were just going through the motions. And maybe, she needed you too. Maybe she needed to meet a man who was honest, both to her and to himself, who knew what was right and what was wrong. You gave her a good look into a world she had only dabbled in before. So, all I am saying is, don't be too harsh with her. The world isn't black and white, good or evil. You know there are lots of shades of gray. You want to think that she should have told you what was going on, that you could have arrested Rickstraw and brought him to justice. But could she really do that without betraying her family's confidences? Wouldn't there still have been an army of cops at Tara's house no matter your intentions? See it from her side of the fence."

Mark wondered where this man got his insight. He had never mentioned that he thought PK should have come to him with her sister's problem, but his boss had stated it as if it was common knowledge. And he was right about not judging her too harshly. She was a product of her environment, and what right did he have to try and change her? But still, he couldn't seem to condone what she may have done. And he wasn't brave enough to ask her.

"I hear what you are saying, and I don't disagree. But I'm still having problems with her possible involvement in a murder. I just can't set it aside."

"And I would be disappointed with you if you could. You're a cop, a good one, and murder is wrong, no matter the justifications. But she's done you another big favor. She has solved your dilemma by electing to leave the country. You don't have to make a decision. She made it for you. And I think she knew the pickle you were in and thought enough of you to leave her world behind, at least for a while. This can't be easy for her either."

Mark let these words wash over him. His mind flashed back once again to the night in the rain, the way she looked at him. She had never told him that she loved him, at least not with words. But those eyes had glowed with affection. She had never promised him anything, but he knew the chief was right; this wasn't easy for her either. And so he asked, "She's invited me to her cabin tonight. Should I go?"

The chief's face drew into a sad smile. "Mark, this is Christmas. Don't spend Christmas by yourself unless you have no choice. You will never feel so alone. You need to go say good-bye, to thank her for what she has done for you, and to allow her the same opportunities. If you don't go, you will regret this for a long time."

Their conversation was interrupted by the squawk of the radio, "A1, Dispatch."

The chief picked up the portable radio that sat on the corner of his desk, "A1, go ahead."

"A1, there's a SO detective at the front door who is requesting to talk to you and A15."

"A1 copies." The chief then turned to Mark, "It appears that the intrepid Detective O'Rourke is here. Just answer her questions. You don't know anything important. Use the conference room for your interview. I'll handle any calls that come in while you two are talking. But then I want to get home and get some sleep just in case I get called out for a fat man in a red suit trying to burglarize a house."

Mark left the chief's office and went to the front door where Detective O'Rourke waited for him. She was wearing her green windbreaker with SHERIFF stenciled on the back. He guessed that was her way of letting him know that this was a business call. He opened the door and led her to the conference room. He offered her coffee and was a little surprised when she accepted. He found a clean mug and filled it with the dark liquid. Normally, he would be worried about how long it had sat there, but the chief was a coffee fanatic, and always kept a fresh pot on hand. And if the chief had brewed the coffee, it was a good cup. They sat on opposite sides of the large table. O'Rourke played with some papers and then looked him in the eyes. He returned her gaze. He wasn't sure what she was trying to accomplish, but he had decided not to go out of his way to help her. He would answer her questions, but he wasn't going to volunteer anything. He owed PK that much. And so they sat in silence.

O'Rourke spoke first, just before the quiet became awkward. "Tell me about your relationship with Celeste. You do know that's not her real name, don't you?"

"I do and so do you. I call her PK. It's short for Peacekeeper. I don't think I have ever called her by her real name. We met at the protest by the mill this last summer. Then I ran into her at the restaurant she works at a bit later. We started spending time together. We're both busy and so it's usually only an hour or two here and there. But I consider those moments precious."

"Have you been to her home?"

"I have."

"How many times?"

"Twice."

"Has she been to your house?"

"No."

"Would you lie for her?" The question was close to an accusation.

Mark paused only briefly, "I might, but I haven't yet." He saw a very brief smile cross the detective's face.

"When did you realize that Tara and …. PK were related?"

"When I entered the house, Tara was only partially dressed. I went into her bedroom to get her some clothes. I saw a family picture that had both sisters in it."

"So, when you interviewed her, you knew she was your girlfriend's sister? Shouldn't you have recused yourself from the investigation?"

"In hindsight, that might have been a good idea. But according to your sergeant, she wasn't going to talk to anyone else. And I would have had to explain why I was unwilling to interview her. That wouldn't have been good for either PK or myself. We were both trying to keep our relationship secret from our families, so to speak."

"Did Tara know about the two of you?"

"I learned later that she did, but I didn't know that at the time."

"So, she was playing games with you? She kind of threw you under the bus."

"I can't blame her. And it is my understanding that she didn't do it on purpose. She underestimated your perception."

"Well, bully for her. Have you seen PK since the search warrant?"

"Yes."

He could see the detective's lips form a very slight sneer as she asked, "When?"

"We had breakfast together this morning."

"Where was that?"

"It's not important."

"Let me be the judge of that. Where did you two have breakfast?"

"it's still not important. No one overheard our conversation."

"Why don't you want to tell me? What are trying to hide?"

"I'm not trying to hide anything. I just don't want you pestering someone who doesn't know anything and probably wouldn't tell you if they did."

"I could tell your boss that you are refusing to cooperate."

"You're going to try and kill my career because I won't tell you where we had breakfast. Fuck you, O'Rourke. Go tell him." Mark paused for a couple of seconds and just before the silence again became difficult, he asked, "Why are you being such a hard ass? Does this style work for you?"

"I'm being a hard ass because you are just answering my questions. I would expect a fellow cop to volunteer what he knows without being asked."

Mark paused to gather his thoughts. This had gone far enough. He was pissed at the detective, but this was getting neither of them anywhere. "O'Rourke, I'm fairly sure that you have loved someone in your life, cared about what happened to them. Whether I love PK or not is a good question, but I do care about her. And if I knew anything that would help you, I might volunteer it, but I don't know anything pertinent to your investigation. PK offered to tell me what she knew, what she had done, but I told her I didn't want to know. And part of the reason I didn't want to know is so that I wouldn't have to tell you. I care about her. I don't want to help get her in trouble. That's your job, not mine. Can you understand that?"

Now it was O'Rourke's turn to pause. A smile formed in her eyes as she finally replied, "Yes, I can understand that. I want to talk to her. Can you help me find her?"

"You had better hurry. She told me this morning that she is leaving the country in a couple of days."

"She's leaving the country? You've got to be fucking kidding me!"

"Nope, that's what she told me."

"You believe her?"

"I have no reason to doubt her."

"Do you know where she is going to be before she leaves?"

Mark hesitated just a second before answering, "I am meeting her tonight at her cabin after I get off work."

"You're meeting her tonight? What for? She's a suspect in a murder investigation."

"I don't know that and neither do you. I'm meeting her to say good-bye. As she would put it, our journey together has finally reached its destination."

The smile had disappeared from O'Rourke's eyes, but it returned again, and her face softened. "That's pretty hippy."

Mark allowed himself to relax just a bit. "Yes, it's kind of hippy, but I'm kind of hippy too. I just cover it up some."

"You really care about this girl? It's not just a sexual thing?"

"O'Rourke, you may find this hard to believe, but we haven't had sex, just some heavy petting."

"Is that going to change tonight?"

"I certainly hope so," he responded with a large grin. He didn't know why he was discussing his sex life with this woman, but he also felt that it was safe. She wouldn't make fun of him or share his confidences. Something about her demeanor made him think that she understood, that perhaps she had been in a similar place at some point in the past.

She was fully smiling now. "I'm sorry that I have been such an asshole about this. When Sergeant Grady walked away from this case, I wanted very much to make something of it, to rub it in his face and show him that I can do the job. So, I have been pushing hard to try and find some traction. But no one is willing to talk to me. My lieutenant has told me that if I don't make some serious progress by the end of the year, that he is going to cold case it. Without a body, I am a bit surprised that he hasn't done so already. Rickstraw was no angel. And it's not like I don't have other work to do. Christmas seems to be the season for the pervs to come out of the woodwork."

She stood up and headed for the backdoor to the station. He followed and walked her out to her car. He was a bit surprised to see that she was driving her personal car and not a County rig. She saw him looking at the license plate. "You don't have to worry about me breaking down the door during your romantic interlude. I'm headed to SoCo to spend Christmas with my family. I'm already late for dinner."

They stood in a cold, light rain, both holding the other's gaze. "You're working this case on your own time?" Mark asked with just a hint of incredulity.

"Yeah. I went by PK's cabin this evening. Her truck was parked in front, but by the time I got around to the rear of the main house, there were no lights on in the cabin. There was smoke coming out of the chimney though. No one answered my knock, but I think she was there. I don't have enough to bring her in if I wanted to. From everything that I have heard, I don't think she would talk to me even if I could pin her down."

"You're right. She wouldn't talk to you. She grew up in the heart of the marijuana world. It's in her DNA not to cooperate with the police if it puts any of her tribe at risk. But Rickstraw was a complete asshole. Why do you want to catch his killer so badly?"

O'Rourke's face became wistful. "I watched you interview Garvey. I could tell that you are good at reading people. So am I, at least I think I am. So, I am going to tell you something that I can barely tell myself. It isn't about catching killers, it's about proving myself. I am the only woman in an office full of A-type personality men. It's ok that I work on sexual assaults and child molestation cases. That's woman's work in the investigation world. But murders, that's a man's job. I am constantly trying to prove that I can do the same job they can, maybe better. I don't get many opportunities though. When Grady walked away from this one because he thought it was a waste of time, I grabbed the chance to prove him wrong and show what I could do. It doesn't help that he was right."

Mark almost felt sorry for her. He extended his right hand. "No hard feelings?"

She took his hand in her own and gave him a firm shake. "No hard feelings."

As she turned to get into her car, Mark added, "If determination is any part of being a good investigator, then I think you will turn out to be one of the best."

She opened the car door but turned to look at him one more time. "Thanks, Coltrane." She paused briefly before adding, "Merry Christmas."

Before he could respond in kind, she had closed the door, started the car, and began to back out of her parking spot. Mark turned back towards his station. He did feel sorry for the detective. This job was hard enough as it was without the drama of stereotype roleplaying.

As Mark entered the station, he found the chief waiting for him. "I'm glad you two worked things out. It sounded like it was getting a bit heated there for a minute or two." He paused and then added, "You two aren't that different you know. Both good at what you do, both driven. She could be a good friend in the future."

Mark only nodded his agreement.

The chief slipped into his coat and headed towards the door. "Merry Christmas, Mark. Just remember to enjoy what the world brings to you. There are no do-overs or mulligans." And with that, he was out the door.

"Merry Christmas, Chief," he responded to the closed door.

Mark gathered his equipment and prepared for his shift. He had no pending paperwork and so rather than sit in the office and wait for the phone to ring, he headed out to his patrol car. He drove in circles, window rolled down despite the inclement weather. Holiday greetings flowed to and from his vehicle as he slowly cruised the side streets. It was always surprising to him how many people were out walking on Christmas Eve. As he returned to the main drag through town, he saw a man walking on the sidewalk. There was something about his walk that looked familiar. And then the man waved to him, signaling him to pull over.

"A15 is being hailed by one, 600 block of Main."

"Roger, A15 is out with one, 600 block of Main."

Mark got out of his car and walked to where the man was waiting for him. He knew that he knew this man, but he couldn't place him. He held a plate of Christmas cookies in front of him. He thrust these forward as Mark got close.

"You don't recognize me, do you?" the man asked. But rather than being offended, the man seemed to be pleased by Mark's failure.

"No, you got me," Mark responded although he was pretty sure that he would remember who this was when it wasn't important anymore.

"I'm Joe McDonald, you arrested me a couple of months ago." He paused briefly, "You took ice cream to my girl, Lizzie, good ice cream."

Recognition came quickly to Mark. It was no wonder that he hadn't recognized the man. His eyes were bright, his skin was clear, and he had gained at least ten pounds. He looked and moved like a healthy young man. "You look good, Joe, like a new man."

"I am a new man, and you helped me become that person. You helped me, more than you know. When you're an addict, you have to hit absolute rock bottom before you can summon the effort to change. I had made some bad choices. I got hooked up with Rickstraw. I owed him a lot of money. But I was so into the dope that I ignored the consequences. Getting arrested was bad, but it was only the tip of the iceberg. And it was your job. You're supposed to arrest people. But when you went to my house to take Lizzie the ice cream, you scared the shit out of her. She was convinced that you were there to tell her that I was in the hospital or the morgue. She let me have it when I got home. It was bad. But it got worse the next morning. She told me that she was never going through that experience again and if I didn't get clean, she was leaving me forever. I loved dope, but I loved Lizzie even more. The thought of her not being part of my life was more than I could fathom. I started going to NA, I got help. It was hard, but Lizzie helped and now I have been sober for 55 days. I don't plan on ever going back."

Mark's smile flowed like warm honey through his core. "Joe, you did this on your own. I didn't do anything."

Joe was shaking his head as Mark uttered these words. "You don't get it. You went out of your way to help someone. It wasn't your intention to scare my girlfriend, but that doesn't matter. You were being human; you were caring about someone else and that is something that people like me don't see, especially from cops."

Mark thought about the grief analogy he had tried to explain to PK, of the pit and the stones. "I think I do understand Joe. I still think that you were the one who pulled yourself out of that hole you had dug for yourself, but I am honored that you think I gave you a hand."

Mark watched as Joe's smile engulfed his whole face. He again thrust the plate of cookies in front of him. "I wanted to thank you in person. I called and learned that you were working tonight. I wasn't sure that I could explain why this was so important to me. I'm thrilled that you get it." He raised the cookies higher, and Mark took them. "I wanted to do something to show my appreciation. I'm not a baker, but cookies this time of year seemed like a good idea, not too presumptuous. Lizzie helped, mainly by laughing at me. There's flour all over our kitchen. They're not real good, but they are edible."

"Thank you, Joe. How is Lizzie?"

Joe's face gushed with pride. "She's doing much better. The morning sickness is gone and there aren't any problems. The baby is healthy. Lizzie's got this rosy glow and she's more beautiful than ever. I'm the luckiest man alive."

"I'm happy for you, Joe. Would you like a ride back home, get you out of the weather?"

"No, thank you. I'd rather walk, but thanks for the offer. I want to thank God for his blessings."

"Ok, Joe. Merry Christmas."

"Merry Christmas, Officer Coltrane. And thanks again for all you have done for Lizzie and me." He turned and walked back the way he had come, his head tilted slightly upwards.

Mark keyed his lapel mike, "A15 is clear."

"A15 is clear."

He got back in his car and placed the cookies on the seat next to him. He had forgotten to pack a lunch and all the stores were closed for the holiday. It looked like the cookies would have to tide him over. Wasn't that what Christmas was all about though, the generosity of others. He bit into one of the cookies. It was a tad bit hard, but tasty, with a hint of cinnamon, and not too sweet. He finished the first and started on a second as he drove in little circles through town. The chief was right, life was what you made of it and right now, it was rather good.

Chapter Twenty

College Town

December 25, 1996, 0220 Hours

The storm front that had come straight across the Pacific and heralded the atmospheric river had moved on. Now a cold front from the Gulf of Alaska was hitting the North Coast. The temperature had dropped twenty degrees, and the raindrops were big and slushy as they hit his windshield and were swept aside by the wipers. He had gone home after work and switched to his old pickup as he had tire chains for it. He didn't need them now but feared that he would in the morning. The forecast was for snow above 1000 feet by dawn and PK's cabin was far above that. Visibility was dropping as he drove up the road that led into the hills above College Town. The clouds lay low, and now he and his truck were enveloped in the softness of the heavens. With no traffic this early on Christmas morning, he drove in the center of the roadway, giving him more time to react as the road wound around the contours of the hillside below the cabin. He was thankful that he was almost there. The dashed yellow line swung to the left and he made the hairpin turn and then slowed to a crawl as he looked for her driveway. And there it was, with her Toyota parked to one side. He eased his Ranger alongside of her four-wheel-drive and turned off the ignition.

He pulled his coat tighter around him. It was cold here and the snow was beginning to stick on the leaves and branches of the nearby trees. PK's truck also had a layer of white slush on the more level surfaces. The light mounted on the corner of the garage was on and he walked around to the back of the house once again and took in the cabin for what was likely to be the last time. There was only candlelight in the window, but there was smoke coming from the chimney. Unlike the previous times that he had been here, he didn't hear any music. He thought about turning around, of just walking away. He knew that sleep was precious. But that wasn't what he wanted, and he was pretty sure that wasn't what PK wanted either. He walked to the porch and climbed the steps. There was no sound, not even the wind blowing through the trees. Big, wet snowflakes were visible as they fell to the ground in front of the kitchen window. He knocked lightly. He counted his heartbeats. They seemed be shaking him to his core. He was just about to knock again when the door opened. And there she was.

Her hair was loose around her shoulders, backlit by the light of the fire in the woodstove. Her face was in dark shadow, but he could feel her eyes upon him. She moved aside to let him in. They had danced this dance before. It was then that he noticed that she wore little more than a pink, silk robe. The cabin was warm, thanks to the raging fire in the stove. She took his coat and hung it on a hook by the door. She held out her hand, palm up and asked, "What music did you bring?"

He handed her two CDs. The decision had not been that hard. The first was the soundtrack to *Forrest Gump;* the music that helped him through the worst of times. The second was what he considered his most romantic music: *Collaboration* by George Benson and Earl Klugh. Both men were master guitarists, and he loved the way they wove acoustic and electric guitar together in melodies. The last track was the love theme from Romeo and Juliet and there didn't seem to be a better song for this night.

She looked at the discs he had provided. She smiled when she saw *Forrest Gump*, but had a more whimsical gaze when she glanced at the second disc. She went to a stereo system that was mounted on the wall above the kitchen table. He had been focused on other things and hadn't really paid it much attention before, but he now noticed that the system was made up of quality components including a large reel to reel tape player. She took the jazz disc out of the case and popped it into a player. George Benson's vocals filled the small cabin. She started to sway gently from side to side. Earl Klugh's guitar joined in a duet. He watched her as she slowly danced, eyes closed, her focus absorbed by the music. He thought about trying to join her, but dancing had never been his thing and he was quite content to simply watch this amazing creature sway before him. And then she stopped, opened her eyes, and looked right at him.

They stood apart in a slightly awkward silence. But that ended when she came to him and wrapped her arms around his neck. His lips found hers and their tongues danced and darted. He broke for air and to look upon this beautiful young woman in front of him. She returned his gaze and they held each other, eyes drinking in the images before them.

And then she broke away completely and retreated into the kitchen area. She opened a cupboard and took down a bottle. She found a glass and silently offered him one too. He shook his head. While it was tempting to join her, he wanted to remember this night for as long as possible and booze was not going to help in that regard. He watched as she poured a couple of fingers into a glass and sipped lightly. As she put the bottle back on the shelf, he saw that it was tequila, but the brand meant nothing to him. She returned to where he stood, glass in one hand and the other around his neck once again. She dipped her tongue into the glass and then once again found his lips with hers. He could feel the sting of the alcohol on his lips and tongue. He pulled her tight against him, their hips locked together, but their backs lightly arched as once again they sought out each other's eyes. He was conscious of her breasts brushing lightly against his chest and he could feel himself begin to grow hard. PK took a sip from her glass and then kissed him again, this time transferring a small amount of the drink. He could feel the burn as it reached the back of his mouth. He backed his head away and was about to speak when she placed her index finger in front of her lips and shushed him. She dipped the same finger in the glass and raised it towards his face. But instead of reaching for his lips, she used her finger to paint the skin below his ear. The rush of his blood was cooled by the evaporation of the booze. He found it highly erotic. Her tongue then painted a different picture on his neck and her teeth nipped at his ear lobe. He cocked his head to the side to give her more room to work. She moved from hairline to shirt collar with just the tip of her tongue sending tingles down Mark's spine.

She backed away and grabbed his T-shirt on both sides just above his hips. She lifted the shirt as he raised his arms, and he felt the fabric gently slide over his face. When he opened his eyes, she was still in front of him with the shirt at her feet. He reached for the edge of her robe, but she brushed his hands away, whispering only, "Not yet, Cowboy."

She arched her back and once again dipped her finger into the tequila. She traced the outline of his nipple. The warmth of her finger, the evaporation of the alcohol, and the testosterone that was flowing through his veins gave him a wide array of sensations. This was followed once again by her tongue as it traced the same route as her finger had. He held her with one hand and ran the other through her hair, gently massaging the nape of her neck and her scalp above. His nose was filled with her aroma: earth, woodsmoke, burnt marijuana, and a heavy dose of musk. How did life get any better?

She stopped torturing his skin and laid her head against his chest. He brought both hands up and gently massaged her shoulders. She took one of his hands and used it to trace her collarbone. He took the hint and used his thumbs to trace the bony ridges from sternum to shoulder, sliding his hands underneath her robe. He felt her quiver slightly under his touch. His hands slid lower, finding the sides of her breasts, her love handles, as diminutive as they were and then the hardness of her hip bones. He used his thumbs once again to trace the top of that ridgeline. She did not push him away this time. Rather she ran her hands through his close-cropped hair and pulled his lips to hers. His hands found the small of her back and the top of her butt cheeks, the knot holding her robe closed a thing of the past. He continued to hold her close as their lips danced, and he massaged the soft flesh of her rear.

And then she pushed him away gently once again and started to work on his belt buckle. She was deft, he was clumsy, but before long they both stood naked in front of each other. Their eyes were locked, their peripheral vision taking in each other's bodies. And then she closed the distance, pushing him gently with her body until the back of his legs brushed up against her bed. She continued to push and when he fell backwards, she joined him. He lay on his back and she straddled him just high enough to keep the important parts separated. He leaned down so that her hair brushed his face, and he could feel her nipples on his chest. They kissed once again.

The rest of the night would fill his memories for years. He would hold onto them tightly. There was the feel of her skin on his, sometimes soft and palpable, sometimes hard and ungiving. There was the feeling of her weight upon him and that of incredible lightness when the roles were reversed, and he could feel her move beneath him. There were fluids, some more viscous than others. Some of these fluids were sweet, all were a bit salty. There were words that found their way to his ears, but most of what he heard were the soft and tender sounds of lovemaking. And then there was the occasional cry, once or twice in pain, like when she bit his ear lobe or raked his back with her nails. But most of the cries were of delight. His nose was filled with the scent of sex until it became overwhelmed. But the thing that he thought he would hold onto the longest was her hair. The texture and feel varied. It was soft, coarse, straight, curly, long, or short depending upon the moment and their relative positions. She used it as another appendage, to massage, to tickle, and to just plain delight him.

The lovemaking seemed to last forever. Perhaps it was matter of minutes, maybe it was hours, he wasn't sure. But at some time in the early morning, completely satiated and spent, he fell into a deep, dreamless sleep. The last thing he remembered, before his eyelids were too heavy to hold open, was the feel of her body next to his, of the warmth they shared. The journey had been special. But the destination had been spectacular.

He awoke with sunlight in his eyes. And then it was gone. He realized that the clouds had broken and now the wind was quickly moving them across the sky. He rolled over and moved his gaze from the open window to the inside of the cabin. PK was across the room in front of her stereo. She wore headphones and seemed oblivious to his consciousness. He lay in bed and watched as she gently swayed to sounds that only she could hear. She was dressed only in the pink robe from the night before and her hair was loose and wild. He was captivated. He could tell that one song had ended and another had begun as her dancing became more energetic and she began to twist and turn. It was during one of these turns that she caught him watching her.

She unplugged the earphones and took them off. Bob Marley's voice rang out asking Mark if he could be loved. She slipped out of the robe and slowly walked to him. His eyes took in all that she was offering, from the triangle of blonde hair centered at the top of her legs, to the flatness of her belly, the slight sway of her breasts as she walked, and her head held high. She knew the reaction this would get, and she was not wrong. She pulled back the covers and once more climbed astride of him. Their morning lovemaking was slow and steady in contrast to the frenetic activity of the night before. He kept his eyes open as did she. They watched each other as they moved in unison, each taking delight as their partner approached, and then found orgasm.

But she didn't settle down next to him. As Diana Ross asked her lover to touch her in the morning and then just walk away, PK climbed from the bed and headed for the shower. He tried to join her, but there was no room in the tiny shower stall. So, he watched as the water beaded on her skin and flowed around the contours of her body. He offered to help her reach some of those hard-to-reach places that he was sure needed cleaning, but she spurned his advances, claiming that she would love to let him help, but once again, she was pressed for time. He helped her dry off when she exited the stall and watched as she quickly dressed. When she had laced her boots, she went to the kitchen table and retrieved two small boxes. One was obviously a cassette tape. The other was smaller and more square in shape. She beckoned him to open it. Inside was a small metal statue of two frogs locked in a kiss. She then handed him the cassette.

"I put this together while you were sleeping. I volunteer at the University's radio station, so I have access to lots of different kinds of music. The tape has some of my favorites and some of yours. I hope the songs remind you of me and the time we spent together. I know they will do so for me."

He looked at the tape case. There was a water painting of a crescent moon and a single star. They were in close proximity, but not touching. The tape was titled "Celestial Bodies." He realized that he was listening to the same tape on the reel to reel as he glanced at the playlist.

"I have something for you too." He walked to where his coat hung next to the door and from a large pocket, removed a framed photo. When Karen had died, he had inherited her camera and often carried it with him when he was in the wilds. Unlike Karen, he didn't like taking pictures of people, but preferred landscapes and the beauty of the natural world. He had been quail hunting earlier in the fall and was headed back to his truck with the sun setting behind him. The light had been low on the horizon and lit up the autumn foliage. He had snapped a single picture without putting much thought into the composure. When he had the film developed, he realized that it was one of the best pictures he had ever taken. And so he wanted to share it with her. He hoped that it was enough; he hoped that it wasn't too much.

She tore open the package and gazed upon the image. He couldn't read her face. But when she finally looked up, he could see what looked like tears in her eyes. She kissed him, gently at first, then more fiercely. But she broke away and took up an envelope that had also been on the table. She handed it to him.

"Open this when I am gone. I wanted to say some things, but I was afraid that my words would fail me when you were in front of me. So, coward that I am, I put them on paper." Diana had long since ended her ballad and now Judy Collins' voice issued forth from the speakers. It was one of his favorite songs, written by Leonard Cohen. How had she known?

I loved you in the morning, our kisses deep and warm
Your hair upon the pillow like a sleepy golden storm

She stood in front of him, coat on, ready to go. He felt the tears start to form. She kissed him once again, gently on the lips and then pulling his head down to hers, on his eyelids. "Listen to the words," was all she said as she turned and walked out the door.

Your eyes are soft with sorrow
Hey, that's no way to say goodbye

Despite Judy's admonition, the tears continued to flow across his cheeks. A dark cloud was overhead, and it had begun to snow again. He watched as the snowflakes caught in her hair. Her boots crunched through a couple of inches of untouched snow. As she reached the corner of the garage, she turned and gave him a tearful half-smile. And then she was gone.

He heard her truck start as he opened the envelope. He pulled out a hand-written note:

Dearest Mark,

If events have transpired as I had ~~planned~~ hoped, I am gone now. It is unlikely that we will meet again, at least not anytime soon. You have thanked me several times for bringing you back to life. And maybe I won't ever understand. But, sweetie, this wasn't all about you. Watching you leave the shell you use to protect yourself from the darkness has been one of the best experiences of my life. I have tasted your tears. I have brought you to the heights of ecstasy. There is a reward there that I don't think you understand. I know that you are ready to move forward with your life. You no longer have a need for me. You will find a woman who can give you what you truly seek, that which I can't and won't provide.

You have shown me what a good, decent man is like and I have realized how self-serving and narcissistic my previous lovers have been. It was not easy to say goodbye. This was not a one-nightstand, another notch in my lipstick case. I fell for you when I wasn't expecting to. I will always remember you; you will always be loved. Goodbye Mark Coltrane. Go out into the world and live.

May you live in love for all of your days and may some of that love be mine.

Celeste

Epilogue

Small Town

November 18, 2019, 1234 Hours

He had spent the morning in court testifying about a domestic violence incident. The District Attorney's Office was trying to send the suspect to prison for an extended period of time. It wasn't just that he had punched his girlfriend and then tried to strangle her. No, in his drunken stupor, he had followed her to a neighbor's house and broken down the door to fight with her protector. After getting hit in the head with a fire poker, he had retreated out the door, with a little help from the neighbor, only to throw a Halloween pumpkin through the living room window. He had then started to throw anything he could lay his hands on, predominately firewood, through the window, striking both the girl's protector and his wife. The suspect had cut his arms badly on the broken glass and he had a headwound from the poker. There had been blood everywhere and they had collected samples of it all. The suspect was claiming that he had been attacked by his girlfriend and the neighbor in his own apartment, had been hit in the head with a brick rather than a poker. But the blood trails suggested otherwise. Mark's testimony had pushed the limits of his memory, one of the many pitfalls of age, but the suspect had been bound over for trial regardless.

Now he sat parked under the freeway where he could watch the stop sign at the end of the freeway offramp. It was the most commonly run stop sign in town. If he sat here, it looked like he was monitoring traffic, when in actuality, he was daydreaming. He found himself doing this more and more often. He would occasionally think about his life, as he was doing now. Overall, he was pretty happy with the way his life had turned out. He had a son that he considered to be the smartest man he had ever met. He was kind, courteous, sensitive, and empathetic. Mark was confident that he would grow to become the decent type of man that he so admired and strived to emulate. He thought about Karen, her death, and how it had shaped him. And he remembered the girl; what was her name? He had called her PK, but what was her real name? Celeste? No, that was what her sister called her. It frustrated him that he couldn't remember. Oh well, it would come to him when he started to think about other things. He had told himself that he would never forget her and now he couldn't even remember her name. But as he recalled that snowy Christmas morning all those years ago, the blood rush to his groin made him realize that he had not forgotten everything. He let himself daydream about days gone by in his youth.

And then the pleasant memory was pushed aside as he saw a newer model, brown, Mercedes sedan flying down the offramp. There was no way that it could stop in time and he hoped that there was no cross-traffic. He threw his patrol car into gear and watched as the Mercedes flew past the stop sign going at least thirty miles-per-hour. His foot hit the throttle as he found the switch that activated his lightbar. Patrol cars had not changed that much in twenty-five years other than now they were often SUVs. The sedan slowed a bit as it entered Main Street and he was easily able to catch up, his lights flashing red and blue in the early afternoon sun. The car turned up a side street and pulled to the curb.

He uttered into his radio microphone, "Dispatch, A1 is traffic, Homer at Main on a brown Mercedes, unreadable plate."

"A1 is traffic, Homer at Main, unreadable plate," came through the speaker. He turned on his portable radio as he got out of the patrol car. As he walked up to the Mercedes, he could now read the license plate that was partially obscured by a cover designed to defeat automatic license plate readers. He smiled as he spoke into the portable radio's label mike, "Dispatch, plate is personalized Edward-Nora-Victor-Ida-Robert-Ocean-Six."

"Roger A1, ENVIRO-6 is clear and current, registered to a last of Jackson out of Weedtown."

His smile grew broader, "A1 copies." And then he was at the driver's side door. The driver had the window rolled down and she turned to look at him. She was still stunningly beautiful. There were some wisps of grey in her hair, but he thought it looked a bit like the last fog evaporating in the morning sun. There were small crows-feet at the corners of her eyes, but the irises were still the bright, cobalt blue of a midday, mountain sky. Her blouse had several buttons undone and her shorts did not cover much of her thighs. She had her license and other papers waiting in her hand.

He heard himself say, "Good afternoon Annabelle." The name had come to him when he wasn't thinking about it. Funny how that worked.

She responded in turn, "Good afternoon Chief Coltrane."

"I was just thinking about you."

"I've been thinking about you for a long time."

He could feel the blood start to flow away from his big brain and towards his smaller, more stupid one. "I stopped you for running the stop sign coming off the freeway. Did you not see it?" he asked trying hard, and mostly successfully to keep his eyes on her face and not the ample cleavage that was visible.

"No, I knew it was there. Sometimes a girl just has to do what a girl has to do. Are you going to arrest me?"

Mark shook his head. He wasn't sure that he had ever pulled over someone who was trying to get pulled over. "No, but I am going to write you a ticket." He took her paperwork, walked back to the rear of his car and quickly started to scribble out the three-part form.

"A1, status?" came through his radio. He had completely forgotten about his dispatcher. She hadn't forgotten about him, but that was what she was paid to do.

"A1 is Code-4, 10-6 cite," he responded.

"Roger, A1 is Code-4, busy cite."

He thought of his dispatcher. Today's was his favorite. She was smarter than she realized, cared more about him than she probably should. Each and every job in law enforcement had their own stresses and it could eat you up if you weren't careful. She was stuck in a small room, crammed full of radio and telephone equipment. She had, arguably, the most important job in law enforcement. He almost never wrote tickets. She would be trying to picture what this driver had done to earn his ire. He figured it was highly unlikely that she would ever learn the truth and her imagination would be much, much worse than reality.

When he completed the citation, he returned to her window and gave her back her documents. He then handed her the citebook and his pen.

"Please sign your name in the box. It's not an admission of guilt, but a promise to appear."

"And what happens if I won't sign in the box?" she asked with a broad smile across her face.

"Well, if you refuse to sign the citation, I am required by law to take you to jail." He felt his blood start to flow from high to low again.

He watched as she took the pen and started to write in the box. However, he realized that it wasn't a signature, but a series of numbers. She handed the book back to him. He looked at the numbers and realized that it was a phone number with a common SoCo prefix.

"Ms. Jackson, you're flirting with me."

"Yes, I am. Are you going to arrest me for that too?" she asked.

He demanded that his body cool its jets. He was too damn old for this. "I don't think it would be a good idea to arrest you right now for anything less than murder. You haven't killed anyone lately, have you?"

Her smile turned from broad to coquette. "No, I haven't killed anyone *lately*." She put heavy emphasis on this last word. "Does that mean that you're not going to arrest me? I thought that you were required to. Are you going to break the law, Chief Coltrane?"

He couldn't help but chuckle. "Every rule was made to be broken with very few exceptions," was his response. "And one of the benefits of being in charge is that I have very few people to answer to when I do break the less serious of those rules. Drive safely, Ms. Jackson."

Now her smile turned slightly more serious. "I'm sorry for the theatrics…., or maybe I'm not, but all I want to do is talk, to catch up on the last twenty-five years. If that leads to something, all the better. If not, then so be it." She pointed at the form in his hand and said, "You know how to find me."

He raised his left hand and wiggled his ring finger, showing her the wedding band that rested there.

As she started the car, she asked, "Does that really mean that much at our age?" And she shifted the car into drive. He stepped back and she eased the car into traffic and out of his life again. Or had she? His mind drifted back to a deck, a rainstorm and a roaring fire. That night had been the largest rock that anyone had ever provided to get him out of that pit. Had she ever really left his life? Would he ever forget her?

He returned to the office. No one was there. He went into his office and sat at his desk. At the bottom of his monitor stand were two metal frogs, still locked in a kiss. He picked up the trinket and caressed the figures gently with his fingers.

Without turning he said, "Alexa, shuffle my Celestial Bodies playlist."

A female voice that he had learned to appreciate spoke from behind him. "Shuffling your playlist, Celestial Bodies, on Amazon Music."

The synthesizers came through the tiny speaker, followed by Annie Lennox's voice.

Here comes the rain again
Falling on my head like a memory
Falling on my head like a new emotion
I want to walk in the open wind
I want to talk like lovers do
I want to dive into your ocean

And he knew that she would always be part of his story. While he might forget her real name, he would never forget what she had done for him. He looked at the citation that he had placed on his desktop. He stared at the address and phone number. And then he twisted the ring on his finger, his mind a swirl of contrasting thoughts and images. His face broke into a toothless grin. He stayed in that posture, mind dancing with the past until Clara, the Department's clerk, came through the back door and asked him if he was alright.

"Just absolutely fucking groovy!" he responded. The Eurythmics finished and Alexa started the next song. Jackson Browne's voice came through the speaker. This song hadn't been on the original playlist the PK had given him all those years ago and he wasn't a huge Jackson Browne fan, but he had heard this song shortly after PK had left the country and the words seemed to almost be written for how he felt. And so, when he had transferred the playlist to digital, he had added it.

She was a friend to me when I needed one
Wasn't for her I don't know what I'd done
She gave me back something that was missing in me
She could of turned out to be almost anyone
Almost anyone...
With the possible exception
Of who I wanted her to be

He played with the frogs like they were a fidget spinner. He could see that Clara was looking at him with just a bit of concern, but he didn't care. Images flashed through his mind; dew drops on blonde eyebrows, magnetic blue eyes, rivulets of rainwater flowing across tawny skin, the warmth that flowed through him as she held him close. He had concentrated on his daydream to the exclusion of Jackson Browne, but now a new verse broke through into his consciousness.

Talk about celestial bodies
And your angels on the wing
She wasn't much good at stickin' around… but
That girl could sing
She could sing…

He stood up, grabbed the citation and headed towards the shredder. *In for a penny, in for a pound,* he thought as he fed the remaining two copies of the form into the spinning teeth of the paper-eater. He returned to his desk and picked up the frogs again. Sometimes the past just needs to stay in your memory where you can polish the rough edges.

About the Author

Jeff Conner studied forestry at UC Berkeley and came to Humboldt County to work in the woods. His career eventually moved to law enforcement and he spent time working patrol, doing marijuana and other drug enforcement, as well as nuisance abatement. He currently works as a small town police chief. In his spare time, when he can find it, he enjoys reading, writing, cycling, photography, computer gaming, and shooting. He feels blessed to live in one of the most beautiful places in the world.

Made in the USA
Las Vegas, NV
28 December 2021

39738751R00134